W9-AVR-224

"You're afraid of me, Wyatt Ledger..."

"Afraid you might fall hard for me and that I might interfere with your burning desire to settle a score for your mother no matter who it hurts."

"You're reading this all wrong, Kelly. I'm just following the lawman's code. A cop never gets personally involved with a woman he's protecting. It makes him lose his edge. Fear has nothing to do with this."

"Prove it."

She stepped right in front of him, so close he could feel her breath on his bare chest. "Kiss me right now and prove you're not afraid." She took his hand and pressed it to her breast.

He lost it then and he kissed her hard, ravaging her lips, exploding in a rush of desire he couldn't have stopped if he wanted to.

JOANNA WAYNE

COWBOY CONSPIRACY

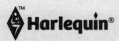

TORONTO NEW YORK LONDON
AMSTERDAM PARIS SYDNEY HAMBURG
STOCKHOLM ATHENS TOKYO MILAN MADRID
PRAGUE WARSAW BUDAPEST AUCKLAND

If you purchased this book without a cover you should be aware
that this book is stolen property. It was reported as "unsold and
destroyed" to the publisher, and neither the author nor the
publisher has received any payment for this "stripped book."

Recycling programs
for this product may
not exist in your area.

ISBN-13: 978-0-373-69592-8

COWBOY CONSPIRACY

Copyright © 2012 by Jo Ann Vest

All rights reserved. Except for use in any review, the reproduction or
utilization of this work in whole or in part in any form by any electronic,
mechanical or other means, now known or hereafter invented, including
xerography, photocopying and recording, or in any information storage
or retrieval system, is forbidden without the written permission of the
publisher, Harlequin Enterprises Limited, 225 Duncan Mill Road,
Don Mills, Ontario, Canada M3B 3K9.

This is a work of fiction. Names, characters, places and incidents are
either the product of the author's imagination or are used fictitiously,
and any resemblance to actual persons, living or dead, business
establishments, events or locales is entirely coincidental.

This edition published by arrangement with Harlequin Books S.A.

For questions and comments about the quality of this book please contact
us at Customer_eCare@Harlequin.ca.

® and TM are trademarks of the publisher. Trademarks indicated with
® are registered in the United States Patent and Trademark Office, the
Canadian Trade Marks Office and in other countries.

www.Harlequin.com

Printed in U.S.A.

ABOUT THE AUTHOR

Joanna Wayne was born and raised in Shreveport, Louisiana, and received her undergraduate and graduate degrees from LSU-Shreveport. She moved to New Orleans in 1984, and it was there that she attended her first writing class and joined her first professional writing organization. Her debut novel, *Deep in the Bayou,* was published in 1994.

Now, dozens of published books later, Joanna has made a name for herself as being on the cutting edge of romantic suspense in both series and single-title novels. She has been on the Waldenbooks bestseller list for romance and has won many industry awards. She is also a popular speaker at writing organizations and local community functions and has taught creative writing at the University of New Orleans Metropolitan College.

Joanna currently resides in a small community forty miles north of Houston, Texas, with her husband. Though she still has many family and emotional ties to Louisiana, she loves living in the Lone Star State. You may write Joanna at P.O. Box 852, Montgomery, Texas 77356.

Books by Joanna Wayne

HARLEQUIN INTRIGUE

*Four Brothers of Colts Run Cross
**Special Ops Texas
‡Sons of Troy Ledger

CAST OF CHARACTERS

Wyatt Ledger—Former Atlanta homicide detective and oldest son of Troy Ledger.

Kelly Burger—Widow with a young child who accepts Wyatt's help when her car is stolen.

Jaci Burger—Kelly's precocious daughter..

Linda Ann Carrington—Kelly's mother.

Cordelia Carrington—Kelly's grandmother, who left her the old Carrington home place.

Dakota, Tyler, Dylan and Sean—Wyatt's brothers.

Viviana, Julie, Collette and Eve—Wives of Wyatt's brothers.

Troy Ledger—Convicted of killing his beloved wife, the mother of his five sons.

Helene Ledger—Late wife of Troy Ledger.

Sheriff Glenn McGuire—Local sheriff and also the father of Dylan's wife, Collette.

Ruthanne Foley—Neighbor of the Ledgers who is romantically interested in Troy.

Senator Riley Foley—Ruthanne's husband.

Emanuel Leaky—Kelly's recently imprisoned former employer.

Luther Bonner—Kelly's former supervisor.

Abby—Owns Abby's Diner and knows everyone in Mustang Run.

Prologue

It was a country club neighborhood. Sprawling brick houses. Manicured lawns. A guard at the gate. The kind of community where people should be resting safely in their beds at 2:00 a.m. on a Sunday.

But in the Whiting home, one resident would never wake up to the smell of morning coffee—the latest Atlanta homicide to drop onto Wyatt Ledger's overflowing plate.

Home murders were the worst, he lamented as he pulled up and stopped behind the two squad cars already parked in the driveway of a columned, two-story brick structure. A lone, bare tree stretched its creaking limbs toward the covered entry. Welcome to paradise gone brutal.

Not that murder was any more horrid or final here than in the backstreets and alleyways where so many of the city's gang and drug-related killings went down. But a home was a person's refuge, the haven from the outside world. Blood seemed so repulsively out of place splattered over pristine surfaces where violence had never struck before.

And home murders hit way too close to the nightmarish memories Wyatt could never lay to rest.

He turned at the squeal of brakes as a blue sedan joined the scene. A second later his partner rushed up the walk behind him, catching up just as he reached the door.

"Be nice if murders occurred during waking hours," Alyssa said as she twisted her skirt until it hung straight over her narrow hips. Even slightly disheveled, she looked good. In any other setting, no one would guess she was as tough and smart as any homicide detective in the city.

"Didn't you have a hot date tonight?" Wyatt asked, but his focus had already moved from Alyssa to the house's surroundings. Lots of trees and shrubs to offer cover for a perp. An alarm-system warning was planted in the front garden. He'd have to check and see if it had gone off.

"Kyle and I went out with friends and didn't get home until after midnight," Alyssa said. "I was sorely tempted to ignore the phone."

"You'd be yelling if you weren't invited to the party."

"Wrong. I hate crime scenes. I love arresting murdering bastards, so I forego sleep."

"I figure we may lose a lot of sleep over this one."

"Why?" Alyssa asked. "What do you know about the crime?"

"Probably the same as you know. Cops were summoned by a 911 call. Found a woman fatally shot. House belongs to Derrick and Kathleen Whiting."

Wyatt opened the unlocked door and stepped inside a high-ceilinged foyer. A multifaceted crystal chandelier dripped light over a marble floor and an antique cherry credenza. Cold air blasted from the air-conditioning unit, though it was already October and in the high sixties outside.

Low voices drifted down the hallway. Wyatt's gut tightened as he strode toward the conversation. He'd been in Homicide six years. This part of the routine never got easier.

He saw the blood first, streams of it flowing away from a body partially hidden by two uniformed officers. Wyatt knew both of the policemen—Carter and Bower. They'd worked night shifts for as long as he'd been with the Atlanta P.D.

"It's ugly," Carter said, stepping back for Wyatt and Alyssa to move in for a closer look. He added a few expletives to make his point.

The victim was lying facedown on the living room floor, wearing a pair of black pajamas. Her feet were bare. She'd been shot in the back of the head at close range. Two bullet entry points were clearly visible.

The wounds were enough to make most men puke. It worried Wyatt a little that he'd become so desensitized to the gore that he didn't pitch his dinner onto the sea of off-white carpet.

"The back door had been jimmied open," Carter said. "The TV is unplugged and pulled out from the wall. Looks as if the victim may have come downstairs and interrupted a burglary in progress."

"Or someone meant it to look that way," Wyatt said. "Did you check the rest of the house for other victims?"

"Yep. All clear. No one else is home. There are men's clothes in the closet in the master bedroom, but only one side of the bed appears to have been slept in. There's another bedroom. Looks as if it belongs to a teenage boy. Slew of baseball trophies on some cluttered shelves and a poster of the Atlanta Falcon cheerleaders on the wall. Dirty clothes piled on the floor. Bed hasn't been slept in."

A boy who'd come home soon to find his mother had been brutally murdered.

A surge of unwanted memories bombarded Wyatt. Events replayed in his mind in slow motion. Staring at his mother's brutally slain body, the pain inside him so intense he'd had to fight to breathe. The panic. The fear. The smell of burning peas. To this day he couldn't stomach the sight or smell of peas.

"Who called the police?" Alyssa asked.

"A neighbor. He said he heard what sounded like gunshots from the Whiting home, but that the alarm system hadn't gone off. When we got here we found the back door wide open, so we came in that way and then unlocked the front door for you guys."

"Have you talked to the neighbor?" Wyatt asked.

"We figured Homicide would want to be the first to do that," Bower said.

The front door banged shut. Either the wind had caught it or someone had joined them. Wyatt's hand instinctively flew to the butt of his weapon.

"Mother."

The voice coming from the foyer was youthful, male and shaky with panic.

Wyatt and Alyssa rushed to the hallway.

"What's wrong?" the boy asked. "Where's my mother?"

The boy looked to be twelve or thirteen, the same age Wyatt had been when his world had exploded. A man in a blue flannel robe stood beside him, his hand on the boy's shoulder. "Has something happened?"

Alyssa flashed her badge. "Alyssa Lancaster, Atlanta P.D. Are you Derrick Whiting?"

"No. My name's Culver. Andy Culver. I live across the street and a few doors down. Josh, here, was spending the night with my son Eric. He woke up and saw the squad cars in front of his house. Was there an accident?"

"There's a problem," Alyssa admitted. "Josh, do you know where your dad is?"

"He's out of town on business."

"Do you have any brothers or sisters?" Wyatt asked. "No."

"Any other relatives who live nearby? Grandparents or maybe an aunt?"

"My grandparents live in Peachtree City. Why? What happened to my mother?" His voice had turned husky, as if he were fighting back tears.

"Why don't we step out on the porch while I explain the situation," Alyssa said.

Explain? As if they were talking about the boy's math homework instead of the end of life as he'd known it. Thankfully, Alyssa was better at talking to the family of a victim than Wyatt was, especially when they were kids.

Wyatt could handle the cold, hard facts of the crime, but he needed the sharp edges of personal boundaries to keep distracting emotions in check.

"Where's my mother?" Josh's voice had become almost a wail.

"I'm sorry, Josh." Alyssa stepped toward him.

Josh broke loose from the cluster and made a run for the living area where his mother's lifeless body lay drenched in blood. Wyatt grabbed for him as he scurried past, but Josh went in for the slide as if he were stealing home. By the time Wyatt reached him, the boy was standing over the body, his face a ghostly white.

Josh trembled, but he wasn't crying yet. That would come later. Now he was in a state of semishock, consumed by the nightmare and ghastly images his mind wouldn't let him accept.

"Mom's dead, isn't she?" His voice broke.

Alyssa slipped an arm around his shoulders as Wyatt took a position that hid the worst of the scene from the boy's line of vision. But nothing either of them could say or do could protect Josh from the horror or the agony that would follow. No one knew that better than Wyatt.

The best Wyatt could do was to apprehend the killer and see that justice was served for Josh's mother. That was a hell of a lot more than anyone had done for Helene Ledger.

Chapter One

Three months later

"The chief wants to see you in his office."

Wyatt looked up at the young clerk who had just stuck her head inside his cubicle. "Did he say why?"

"No, just that he wants to see you."

Wyatt shoved the letter he'd been sweating over into a folder and pushed his squeaky swivel chair back from a desk piled high with case files. He picked up the folder for the Whiting case. He hadn't even finished his written report yet, but he was sure last night's developments would be the topic of the chief's discussion.

He wouldn't be thrilled that Derrick Whiting would not be standing trial for the murder of his wife. But neither would he be walking the streets a free man, with insurance money in the bank and the sexy mistress in his bed.

Whiting had shot himself last night when Wyatt and Alyssa had shown up at his door, arrest warrant in hand. Fortunately, Josh was not there to witness the event. He'd moved in with his grandparents over a month ago.

Alyssa caught up with Wyatt just before he reached the chief's door. "So you were summoned, too."

"Yeah."

"Think Dixon's pissed that we couldn't stop the sick bastard from killing himself?" she asked.

"I'm sure he'd have preferred to have the guy stand trial, but it is what it is."

The door was open. Martin Dixon waved them both inside. He stood and moved away from his desk to welcome them. He wasn't exactly smiling. He never did. But his eyes and stance said it all. He was glad this was over.

"Hell of a job! Both of you. I wish we could have brought Whiting in to stand trial, but I can see why he took care of his own death sentence. And if he hadn't, the evidence you've collected would have guaranteed a conviction. No juror in his right mind would have let him off."

"It's the jurors not in their right minds I always worry about," Alyssa said. "But thanks for the kudos."

"The mayor called this morning," the chief continued. "Said to tell both of you how grateful he is for the way you handled the investigation. He wanted to congratulate you himself, but he's getting ready for a joint press conference he's giving with me in about an hour."

Wyatt grimaced. "You're not going to thank us by making us spoon-feed the details to the media sharks, are you?"

"No. The mayor and I will make statements. Louis will handle the questions about the case, but I need both of you to brief him."

"That, I can handle," Wyatt said.

Louis was in charge of APD public relations and he

had a way of feeding the media just enough to keep them happy without releasing any gratuitous details.

"Anyway, good work," the chief said again.

"Thanks," Wyatt said. "Just doing my job, and I'm certain the guy who ate the bullet was guilty as sin."

Wyatt and Alyssa had eaten and slept that case for three months. The murder had been carefully planned, and *almost* perfectly executed to make it look like a startled burglar had committed the crime. But Derrick had made a couple of fatal errors. Most murderers did.

Thankfully, Derrick Whiting was Josh's stepfather of just over two years and not his biological father. Josh admitted they'd never been close, though Derrick had painted a picture of perfect family harmony to his co-workers.

At least now Josh wouldn't have to live with the knowledge that his real father had killed his mother in cold blood. He wouldn't be forced to endure the cruel taunts of schoolmates for being a murderer's kid or have to wonder if the evil that possessed his father was buried deep in his own DNA.

"You're both up for a promotion," the chief said. "I've decided to skip a few bureaucracy hurdles and move that along."

"Now you're talking," Alyssa said.

The announcement caught Wyatt totally off guard. Great for Alyssa, but so much for the letter of resignation he'd been laboring over for the past hour.

"Is this a problem for you, Wyatt?" Dixon said, obviously picking up on Wyatt's discomfort.

"Not exactly a problem, but…" Might as well blurt this out. The decision was made. "I appreciate the promotion offer, but I'm turning in my resignation."

The chief looked stunned. Wyatt refrained from

making eye contact with Alyssa. He'd planned to tell her first. That was partner protocol, but news of the promotion took this out of his hands.

"When did you decide this?" Dixon asked.

"A couple of weeks ago, but I've been thinking about it for quite a while. I planned to see the Derrick Whiting case through before I talked to anyone about it."

"You should have come to me sooner. Whatever the problem is, I'm sure we can work it out."

"My leaving has nothing to do with department or the work," Wyatt added quickly. "Hell, this place is home. But I need a change. I've been with the APD ever since I dropped out of college and signed on as a rookie cop."

"What kind of change? If it's a move out of Homicide, we can—"

"I'm moving back to Texas," Wyatt said, hopefully ending the discussion.

Dixon looked skeptical. "To go into ranching with your family?"

"I doubt I'll live on the ranch," Wyatt explained, "but I've got unsettled business in Mustang Run and it's time I take care of it."

"Does this have to do with your mother's murder?"

"That's a big part of it," Wyatt admitted.

"Are you sure you've thought this through?"

"I'm sure," Wyatt assured him. He'd thought of not much else for most of his life. It was the reason he'd become a cop. He'd put it off as long as he could.

The chief shook his head, his expression making it clear he thought the move was a big mistake. "You said once that your brothers are all convinced of your father's innocence. I doubt they'll appreciate you stirring up trouble. And he's served seventeen years of a sentence. That's more than a lot of convicted perps serve when there isn't the slightest doubt that they're guilty."

"I'm not going after my father. I'm going after the man who killed my mother. If my father is innocent, I'll prove that beyond a doubt. If he's guilty, then I'll just have to deal with that. My brothers are grown men. They'll have to do the same."

"I hate to say it, but I can see where you're coming from, Wyatt. And I don't doubt for a second that you'll find the answers you're looking for."

"I hope that confidence is justified."

"Keep me posted. And as long as I'm heading up the force, there's always a place for you if you decide to come back."

"I appreciate that."

"When do you plan to leave?"

"My caseload is as caught up as it will ever be, so I'd like to clear out as soon as you replace me."

Dixon nodded. "The department will miss you."

"I'll miss being here."

Talk went back to the Whiting case, but the celebratory tone of the meeting had shifted. Wyatt, usually the first to make a wisecrack to alleviate the tension, could think of nothing to say. He loved his job, but he had to do this.

And he could use a change of scenery. His apartment walls were starting to close in around him. He needed a taste of wide-open spaces, hilly pastures and the quiet fishing spots Dylan, Sean and now Dakota were always talking about.

That didn't make going back to Mustang Run and Willow Creek Ranch any easier.

As soon as they stepped into the hallway, Alyssa

poked him in the ribs. "When exactly did you plan to hit me in the head with this?"

"At the last possible moment, so I wouldn't have to listen to you whine and lecture," he teased. "And don't poke me with those bony fingers."

She poked him again. "You'll go crazy in the Podunk town of Horse Run."

"*Mustang* Run. And I don't plan to be there forever."

"No, just long enough to cause trouble," Alyssa quipped.

"And I'm talented at stirring the pot, so that shouldn't take too long."

"Your dad's already spent seventeen years in prison before being released on a technicality. He's reunited with four of his five sons, even Tyler who's still on active duty in Afghanistan. He's a beloved grandfather. Have you ever considered just leaving well enough alone?"

"I'm not planning to go down there and string him up from the nearest tree. Troy claims he's looking for Mother's killer. I aim to help him."

"Oh, right, the good son. You can't even call him Dad."

Wyatt stopped walking and made eye contact. "Are you telling me you wouldn't feel the same if your mother had been murdered?"

"Okay, point made. But I'll miss you, partner. Worse, I'm selfish. Now I have to adjust to someone new. I'll probably get one who sweats profusely or passes gas in the car, or heaven forbid, treats me like a woman."

"He won't make that mistake but once."

She smiled as if that were the ultimate compliment. "Do me a favor while you're out there with those rattlesnakes and cow patties, Wyatt."

"Send you a snakeskin?"

"Don't even think about it. But if on the off chance you find a woman who can put up with you, don't push her away like she's been living with a family of skunks, the way you did everyone I tried to fix you up with."

"I'll keep that in mind."

"You know what's wrong with you?"

"I don't like skunks."

"You're afraid of falling. As soon you think you might like some woman, you make up excuses for why it won't work. She's too smart. She's not smart enough. She has cats. She has kids. She doesn't like cats or kids."

"You should get better friends to fix me up with."

"You may as well admit it. You're afraid of relationships."

"Shows how smart I am. Do you know the divorce rate among cops?"

"One day you'll meet a woman who'll knock you for such a loop you won't be able to walk away. I hear Texas is full of women like that."

"Could be." But a woman was the last thing he needed now. Texas and reuniting with Troy Ledger would be challenge enough. And now that the decision was made, he needed to move on. With luck, he'd be on the road by the middle of January.

He traveled light. That was just one of the advantages of never putting down any deep roots or acquiring things like mortgages or a wife.

He had no intention of changing that.

"It's the fuel pump, Mrs. Burger. It's going to have to be replaced."

Kelly groaned. She had another four hours to drive

and it was already after three. Plus, the weather forecast for tonight was a line of severe thunderstorms preceding a cold front moving in from the northwest.

The mechanic yanked a red rag from his back pocket and rubbed at a spot of grease on his arm that defied his removal efforts. "I can get to it first thing in the morning. And I'll be glad to give you a ride now to the nearest motel."

"I really need to get back on the road today. I'll pay extra if you can fix it this afternoon."

"I'm not sure how quickly I can get the part. I might be able to just run over to Mac's Garage and pick it up or I might have to have one shipped in."

Just her luck to have her car break down in a small town. "Can't you have someone drive to the nearest town with a Honda dealer and pick one up? I'll pay his overtime and buy his gas."

Jaci tugged on Kelly's skirt. "Can we go now, Momma?"

"Not yet, Jaci." She struggled to keep the frustration from her voice. She couldn't expect a five-year-old to understand why they were just standing around waiting instead of off on the adventure she'd been promised. Jaci had been such a trooper over the last twelve months when their lives had been in serious upheaval.

"Let me see what I can do," the young mechanic said.

He returned to the small waiting area ten minutes later, this time smiling.

"I found a fuel pump that I can have here in under an hour. If we don't run into problems, you can be on your way just after dark."

"Super." They'd arrive in Mustang Run too late to accomplish anything tonight, but at least she'd be at the new house when the moving van arrived in the morning. Not actually a new house—just new to her. Actually it was older than her grandmother who'd willed it to her. But it would offer Kelly a new start after her year from hell.

Not that she had a clue what shape the house would be in. It had stood empty for over a year now and the man who'd been managing the property was visiting his son in California.

All he'd told her over the phone was that the house would need an ample application of soap and elbow grease and paint. She'd decided to move in and fix it up one room at a time as she found the time and the money.

She had some savings but not enough for major repairs. Her husband's medical bills had taken most of it before he died three years ago. And last year, she hadn't earned a dime.

"I'm hungry, Momma," Jaci said, though Kelly suspected she was more bored than anything else.

"There's a McDonalds's out on the highway," the mechanic offered. "I can give you a lift over there if you'd like and pick you up when your car's ready. It's got a nice play area."

Jaci jumped around excitedly. "McDonald's. Please, Momma. Please."

Hours at a McDonald's surrounded by squealing kids and the odor of fries—or sitting here rereading for the twentieth time the two storybooks Jaci had brought with her in the car.

That was a no-brainer.

"That would be terrific," Kelly agreed. Jaci could play off some of her energy, have the chicken nuggets she loved and then she'd likely sleep all the way to the

Hill Country. They'd be back on track and hopefully to Mustang Run before the predicted thunderstorms set in.

Surely nothing else could go wrong today.

Chapter Two

Large drops of rain splattered the windshield as Wyatt pulled off the highway and next to one of the gas pumps at a 24-hour truck stop. Eighteen-wheelers lined the truck parking area off to the right, the drivers no doubt sleeping soundly in their fancy cabs.

He was the only gas customer and the parking lot in front of the café was empty except for a motorbike that looked as if it had seen its best days years ago, and a snazzy new Corvette.

Wyatt climbed from his brand-new double-cab pickup truck, his going-away present to himself for trading a job he loved for a reunion with his father.

All he owned was either tossed into the backseat or stored in the truck's bed beneath the aluminum cover. That included the fancy rod and reel the other homicide cops had presented him with as their going-away memento.

Stretching to relieve the kinks from his muscles, Wyatt massaged the stiff tendons in his neck. The beers he'd enjoyed with his buddies last night had left him with just enough headache pain to dull the fun of hitting the road.

The splatters became a pelting downpour as he filled

his gas tank. A gust of icy wind almost blew his black Stetson off his head. He tugged the hat lower with his free hand.

Just as he was returning the fuel handle to its cradle, a late model Honda Accord pulled up across from him and a woman stepped out.

The wind was blowing so hard now that the sheltering canopy above them did little to keep them dry. She pulled a denim jacket tight and glanced around nervously.

He tipped his hat. "Rough night for traveling."

"Yes. I was hoping the rain would hold off for another hour," she said, cautiously avoiding eye contact as she unscrewed her gas tank.

There was no one in the passenger seat, but he spotted a little girl in the backseat. Her face was pressed against the window as she peered at him. She opened the door for a better look.

"Don't get out of the car, Jaci. It's cold and you'll get wet." When the girl closed her door, the woman quickly locked it with the remote on her key.

"You're getting wet, too," Wyatt said. "Why don't you let me finish gassing up for you and you and the kid make a run for the café before it gets any worse?"

"We're not going in. And thanks for the offer, but I really don't need any help." Her tone and stare clearly told him to back off.

Smart woman. He was harmless, but plenty of men weren't. And a woman and a kid traveling alone would make an easy target for some of the perverts he'd dealt with.

If he was still carrying his APD identification, he could probably reassure her, but he was no longer a cop, at least not officially.

"I'd give the rain a few minutes to slack off before I hit the road again. Just a suggestion," he said, tipping his hat again.

He headed inside for a cup of coffee as the wind and rain picked up in intensity. He was less than thirty miles from Mustang Run but in no hurry to get there. He'd decided about forty miles back that he'd check in to one of the town's two motels for the night and then drive out to the ranch in the morning.

He needed a good night's sleep before he faced Troy.

Troy Ledger, convicted of murder, but still claiming his innocence. Wyatt hoped to God he was, but he'd read and reread the trial notes so many times he knew every last detail. If he'd been on that jury, he'd have come to the same conclusion they had. Guilty of murder in the first degree.

That was the Troy he'd be facing. But it was the other Troy he had been thinking about ever since he'd crossed the Texas line.

The father who'd chased monsters from his bedroom, taught him to ride a horse and a bike. Given him his first pony. The father who'd stayed with him all night when that pony had been so sick they thought they might have to put her down.

Wyatt stamped the water from his worn Western boots and made a stop at the men's room before entering the café proper.

"C'mon in," the waitress welcomed when he finally stepped into the main area of the café. She looked to be in her mid-thirties, blonde, with heavy, smudged eye makeup.

"You made it just in time," she said. "Sounds like a whopper of a storm kicking up out there."

"Is this your usual January weather?" he asked.

"No, but nothing about the weather's predictable in this part of Texas. One day you'll be in shorts, the next day you'll be wearing sweats. Where are you from?"

"Texas originally, but I've lived in Georgia for most of my life."

"Welcome back to the Lone Star State."

"Thanks." He shed his jacket and dropped it to one of the counter stools.

She handed him a plastic-coated menu. "You looking for dinner or just coffee and a warm, dry spot to wait out the storm?"

"Both." He checked out her name tag. "I'll start with a cup of black coffee, Edie."

"The cook's already gone for the night," she said as she poured the coffee and set it in front of him. "I can fix you a burger or a sandwich and fries. I can do most of the breakfast items, too. There was chicken tortilla soup, but a couple of truckers finished that off about thirty minutes ago."

"Whatever you're cooking now smells good."

"I'm making the guy in the back corner a grilled ham-and-cheese sandwich. I recommend it."

"Then I'll have that."

"You got it."

Wyatt glanced at the only other customer. He was bent over a road map that he'd spread across the narrow table. His hair was shaggy and looked like it hadn't been washed in days. His jeans were faded and frayed at the hem. Heavily tattooed muscles bunched beneath a wife-beater T-shirt, and there was a wicked scar at his collarbone.

He might be a perfect gentleman with a spotless record, but he was the kind of guy who always courted a cop's attention.

But Wyatt was no longer a cop. He turned his attention back to the front of the café. The rain slashed against the huge front windows now, and he thought of the woman in the Honda again. If she was trying to drive in this deluge, she was in for trouble. Visibility would be reduced to a few feet.

The bell above the front door tinkled. Wyatt looked up as the woman who'd said she wasn't coming in herded the kid inside and toward the restrooms on the right. Hopefully that meant she'd decided to sit out the storm here.

A loud clap of thunder rattled the doors and the lights blinked off and on.

Edie leaned over the counter in front of him. "I'm sure glad you stopped in. I get spooked if I'm alone or with only one customer when the power goes off. Normally if I yell, any number of truckers would come to my rescue, but they'd never hear me in this storm."

"Is the guy sitting in the back a regular?" Wyatt asked.

"Never seen him before." She leaned in closer. "Hope to never see him again. The way he looks at me gives me the willies. That's another reason I was glad to see you walk in. You look like a guy who can handle trouble."

"Only when trouble throws the first punch."

She smiled and stuck a paper napkin at his elbow. "Storms lure in lots of strangers, especially when the rain is falling so hard you can't see to drive."

Wyatt kept his gaze on the front of the café until the woman and kid came out of the restroom area. The woman looked around and met his gaze for one quick second before leading her daughter to a table at the front of the café.

The waitress sashayed over to them, starting up a new conversation about the storm.

"Just black coffee for me and a glass of milk for my daughter," he heard the woman say once they got around to the order.

"Sure thing. Are you traveling much farther tonight?"

"Just to Mustang Run. I thought I had enough gas to get there, but then the gauge dropped so low I was afraid to chance it."

"Good that you stopped and came in," Edie said. "One of my regulars ran his truck off the road last time we had a gully washer like this."

"We're moving to my great-grandmother's old house," the kid said excitedly. "It has a big yard."

"Lucky you. Is your daddy going to work in Mustang Run?"

"My daddy got sick and he's in heaven," the little girl said. "But I have a gramma Linda Ann in Plano. She's a schoolteacher. At a college."

So the woman was a widow, Wyatt considered. And she and her daughter were moving to the same small town as he was, on the same night.

Alyssa would claim it was serendipity and that he should go right over and introduce himself. But then Alyssa also believed that throwing pennies in the fountain in the courtyard of her favorite restaurant would help her meet the perfect man. If not, Facebook would.

"You're going to love Mustang Run," Edie said to the little girl. "I live about thirty minutes in the opposite direction, but I go into Mustang Run every year for the Bluebonnet Festival Dance. The locals are really friendly." She turned to the woman. "And the cowboys are *sooo* cute."

"I'm not looking for a cowboy."

Wyatt hooked the heels of his Western boots on the stool's rung. That ruled him out. Not that he worked with cows, but he was a cowboy in his soul.

"Where are you moving from?" Edie asked.

"East of here."

You couldn't get much more evasive that than, Wyatt thought. His cop instincts checked in and he wondered if she might be on the run—from the police or perhaps an unwanted lover.

"We're getting a cat," the little girl said.

"That will be nice," Edie said. "I had a cat when I was young. I named it Princess."

"I'm naming mine Belle. That's a princess name."

"It is. I like that."

"My name is Jaci."

"I like that, too. Now I better get back to my grill before I burn the ham."

The thunder was now a constant growl in the background and the pounding on the metal roof sounded like hailstones. The lights blinked again as Edie pulled sliced tomatoes, lettuce leaves and jalapeños from a small built-in refrigerator beneath the counter.

Wyatt shifted on the stool so that he had a better view of the woman at the front table without staring obviously. His mind automatically sized her up the way he would a suspect. The hair was strawberry blond, clean and shiny. It was cut short and in wavy layers that flipped about her chin. She had a cute nose that turned up ever so slightly on the end.

Nice breasts. Slender hips—he'd noticed those when she was pumping gas. Full lips. Great smile—when she smiled.

Okay, so maybe he was noticing her more like a

woman than a suspect. She did intrigue him, maybe because she was showing absolutely no interest in him.

She looked up, saw him watching her and shot him that same back-off stare she had aimed at him outside.

Once Edie put his sandwich in front of him, his concentration turned to the food. When he did look up, he caught the guy at the other end of the bar eyeing Jaci's mother. Wyatt couldn't fault him for noticing an attractive woman. He'd done the same.

But the way this guy was looking at her bothered Wyatt. He could see why the waitress felt uncomfortable around him.

Wyatt felt that copper's itch to find some reason to ask for the man's ID. He'd like to check him out and see if he had a record or an outstanding warrant for his arrest.

A few minutes later, the guy paid his tab, stood and swaggered toward the door. He stopped near the woman at the table and rested his right hand on his groin area, leering until the woman looked up. She glanced away quickly.

Wyatt's muscles clenched. Badge or not, he wasn't going to let the slimy weasel intimidate a woman while he was here to stop it.

But then the guy turned and strode out of the café and into the full fury of the storm.

By the time Wyatt had finished his sandwich and a second cup of coffee, the steady pelting against the roof had finally slacked off. The woman and kid were already pulling on their jackets. They left as Wyatt paid his tab.

He'd just shrugged into his own jacket when he heard the piercing wail. Adrenaline rushed his veins.

He shoved his way out the door, his instincts already kicking in and ready for whatever he might find.

Anything except this.

Chapter Three

The woman from the diner had shoved a motorbike to the pavement and was kicking the frame like she was attacking a hungry grizzly. Had it been a grizzly, the bear would likely be losing the battle.

"What's the problem?" he asked.

Her hands flew to her hips. "That hooligan stole my car."

Wyatt looked around. True enough, there was no sign of the Honda she'd been driving earlier.

"Don't just stand there," she demanded. "Do something."

"Looks like you have the bike subdued," he quipped.

"Not help with the bike. My purse is in that car. All my money's in it. He has my computer. A box of Jaci's favorite toys." She threw up her hands in frustration. "And half of our clothes!" She slammed the heel of her stylish boot into the bike's frame again.

The hooligan in question had a good half hour head start. With no idea which direction he'd gone in, chances were slim Wyatt could chase him down in his pickup truck.

"What in holy tarnation are you doing to my bike?"

This time it was the waitress's shrill voice that cut through the damp air.

The woman threw up her hands. "*Your* bike? I thought it belonged to the man who stole my car."

"That creep who was in the café stole your car?"

"Apparently."

"I knew he was up to no good the second he walked in. I figured he was just hanging around waiting for the power to go off so he could clean out the register."

Wyatt made the 911 call while the women righted the downed bike and the attacker apologized profusely for the damage her boot had inflicted.

The kid ran over to Wyatt. "Call the police and the game warden," she squealed. "That man stole my toys and my books."

Three near-hysterical females was downright scary. The light rain that was still falling did nothing to settle them down. At least the kid had sense enough to move to the cover of the aluminum canopy over the door after she put in her order for cops.

"Ladies," Wyatt announced when he'd finished the call. "A deputy is on the way. Let's go back inside and calm down."

"Easy for you to say," the woman snapped. "You have your truck."

No doubt because the thief didn't realize Wyatt had a couple of loaded pistols inside. Wyatt stopped at the Corvette parked in the lot as the three women marched inside.

If the guy hadn't been riding the motorbike, he must have been driving this. Ten to one it was stolen, as well. But there was nothing he could do about it until a deputy showed up.

Back in Atlanta, he'd have made a few calls and

had local cops and the state police already on the lookout for the stolen Honda. He'd have run a license-plate check on the Corvette. He'd have assumed control instead of waiting for a deputy.

Already he missed his life.

KELLY TOOK A DEEP BREATH and struggled to think rationally. Instead, she plunged into the frightening abyss of "what ifs." What if the creep had been the one pumping gas when she was? What if he'd knocked her to the pavement and stolen the car with Jaci inside it? What if she'd walked out while he was hot-wiring the ignition and he'd shot Jaci or her or both of them?

When she looked at it that way, the loss of her car and her belongings didn't seem nearly so horrific. But still, she was fed up with being criminals' prey. It was as if she wore a sign on her back that said *victim*.

"I'll start a fresh pot of coffee," Edie offered. "You never know how long we'll have to wait for a deputy in this weather."

Kelly and Jaci slid into one side of the narrow booth. Not unexpectedly, the cowboy slid in opposite them. Fortunately, he seemed to be taking command of the situation. Good that someone was, since she'd flown into a rage out there instead of thinking logically.

He was quite a hunk. Not that she hadn't noticed that earlier, but now she actually let her gaze linger on the rugged planes and angles of his face. He couldn't be many years older than she was, if any, but he had an edge about him and an aura of self-confidence.

She liked his hair—short but rumpled and dry—where hers was wet and dripping, thanks to the Western hat he'd just tossed to the booth behind them. His dark brown locks were streaked with coppery highlights, the artistic work of the sun.

But his eyes were the real draw. Mesmerizing. Piercing, but not threatening. The color of the coffee she could smell dripping through the pot.

"I think we should introduce ourselves," he said. "I'm Wyatt Ledger."

"Good to meet you, Wyatt, though I would have preferred to meet under better circumstances. I'm Kelly Burger."

It was a relief to finally use her real name again. Maybe one day she'd even be able to get past the fears she'd lived with for nearly twelve months. She extended her hand and when his wrapped around hers, the tingle of awareness danced through her. She pulled her hand away too quickly. Subtlety was not her strong suit.

She looked down at her daughter, thankful to break away from Wyatt's penetrating gaze. "This is Jaci."

The cowboy's lips split into a wide grin. "Hi, Jaci."

Attacked by one of her rare cases of shyness, Jaci twirled a finger in her hair and looked down at the table. It was well past her bedtime, and even though she'd slept some in the car, she was running out of steam.

Jaci pulled her short legs into the seat with her and finally looked at Wyatt. "Can you take us to our new house?"

"It's okay, Jaci," Kelly assured her. "The police will see that we get home tonight."

"Actually, I heard Jaci say earlier that you're going to Mustang Run," Wyatt said. "That's also where I'm heading, so I can give you a lift if you'd like."

The coincidence set off a warning bell in her head. For all she knew Wyatt could be as bad as the rotten thug who'd stolen her car. Boots and a cowboy hat didn't mean he was the real thing. "Do you own a ranch near Mustang Run?"

"My family does. I was a homicide detective with the Atlanta Police Department until yesterday. Now I guess I'm a freeloader."

"You're a cop?"

"*Was* a cop. Guess it doesn't say much for my detective intuition that I let the guy just walk out of here and steal your car. The fact that he left in the middle of a pouring rain should have tipped me off he might be up to no good, especially since I figured the motorbike was his, too."

"Why did you leave the force?"

"Personal reasons."

That she understood, the same way there were a lot of questions about her life she wouldn't want to go into with a stranger. Or with family for that matter. She hadn't even fully explained the year's disappearing act to her mother. There had been no reason to worry her. Kelly had been frightened enough for both of them.

"If you're a detective, you must know the routine. What happens when the deputy shows up?"

"He'll ask questions about the car. You'll answer the ones you can and then he'll fill out a police report."

"I know the license-plate number. Everything else, I'll have to get from my insurance agent. That may have to wait until morning. Hopefully, I'll have the car back before then."

"I wouldn't count on that."

"Why not?" Her frustration spiked again. "They will look for it, won't they? That's their job."

"That's *one* of their jobs. I don't know how they prioritize around here, but car thefts are not top priority in the big city unless they involve force, weapons or kidnapping."

Panic swelled again. "I need that car. It has my purse with my wallet in it."

"How did you pay your tab in the restaurant?"

"With the credit card I used for buying gas. After swiping it, I'd stuck it in the front pocket of my jeans."

"Did you leave your purse in the front seat? If so, that might have been the lure that made him choose your Honda over my new truck."

"I wasn't that stupid. I put it in the trunk, but there were personal items in the backseat and the sleeping bags Jaci and I were going to sleep on tonight."

"Where exactly were you planning to spread sleeping bags in a storm?"

"On the floor in my house. The moving van with my furniture won't arrive until tomorrow."

"If you have other credit cards, I'd suggest you cancel them at once."

"I don't." She wouldn't have this one had the FBI not obtained it for her. Her credit slate had been wiped clean a year ago and all accounts closed.

"Is there a key to your house in your purse or somewhere else in your car?"

"No, fortunately, I put the house keys on the ring with my car keys earlier today."

"What about your phone?" Wyatt asked.

"It's in the car. No... Wait. It's in my pocket. I forgot it was there. I could have called 911 myself. But my computer is in the trunk."

"What else is in the car?"

"There's a folder with information from the phone company, the electric power company, the natural gas company. The house I'm moving into has been empty for a year. I had to have all the utilities reconnected."

She blinked repeatedly, determined to hold back a surge of tears that was gathering behind her lids. This was no time to cry. She worked to revive the fury that would keep her from showing weakness.

Jaci's head drooped and came to rest against Kelly's shoulder. The darling had fallen asleep. At least she wouldn't see if salty tears started spilling from her mother's eyes.

"I can spread my jacket on that booth behind us if you want to lay her down," Wyatt offered.

"Thanks. I would appreciate that."

She lifted Jaci while he fashioned the makeshift bed. Jaci was so tired she barely stirred as Kelly leaned over and carefully laid her down. The masculine smell of leather and musky aftershave emanating from Wyatt's jacket was strangely reassuring. It had been a long time since she'd had a man help her put Jaci to bed.

Only this wasn't a bed. It was a faded and worn plastic booth in a truck stop. And Wyatt was a stranger who just happened to get caught up in her routinely disastrous life. A stranger who'd likely cut out and run as soon as the deputy arrived.

Who could blame him? Though to be fair, he had offered to drive her into Mustang Run.

Wyatt walked over to the counter where Edie was pouring steaming coffee into large white mugs. Kelly joined him. Before it had cooled enough to take her first sip, the door opened and two men in khaki uniforms with pistols strapped to their hips stepped inside. The law had arrived.

Still, she had the sinking sensation that her problems in moving to Mustang Run were just beginning.

WYATT SIZED UP the two officers. The older one was the sheriff. He looked to be in his midfifties, about the age of Wyatt's father. He was flabby around the middle with weathered skin from years of Texas sun and wind. His eyelids sported a drooping layer of baggy skin.

Yet he had an air about him that suggested he was in control and you'd best not put that to the test.

The second was a deputy. He was significantly younger, probably late twenties. The bottoms of his pants were caked in fresh mud, likely from working a vehicle accident during the storm.

The older man walked over to the counter. "What's this about a car being stolen from the parking lot, Edie?"

Obviously, they knew one another.

"Can you believe it? Some slimeball jerk who stopped in just before the storm hit left in the woman's car. And her with a kid. The gall of some creeps."

"You saw him drive off in the car?"

"No," Edie admitted. "But right smack in the middle of the worst of the storm, with the lights flickering and the power threatening to go at any second, the badass made a suggestive comment as I refilled his coffee cup."

"And you didn't dump the rest of the pot on him?" the younger deputy asked.

"I told him to go screw himself. He paid his tab, no tip, of course. Then he walked out without a word to anyone and drove off in this lady's car." She pointed toward Kelly and then propped her hands on her hips. "I should have at least spit in the slimy bastard's coffee."

"If you still have coffee, Brent and I could use a cup."

"No spit," Brent teased. "I'm armed."

"You'd deserve it, since you haven't stopped by in weeks." She smiled and cut her eyes flirtatiously.

The older man directed his attention to Kelly. "I'm Sheriff Glenn McGuire. Brent Cantrell, here, is my deputy. Sorry about the car, but we'll do what we can to get your vehicle back."

Sheriff Glenn McGuire. Wyatt recognized the name at once. The infamous sheriff had been the one who'd investigated the murder case against Wyatt's father and then made the arrest. He'd been a deputy back then. His arrest of Texas's infamous wife killer no doubt helped propel him to the position of sheriff. He'd held the position ever since.

Oddly, McGuire was practically part of the Ledger family now and apparently a capable sheriff. He'd helped out Wyatt's brothers on several occasions. Danger and mishaps had plagued the sons of Troy Ledger over the past year and a half since Troy had been released from prison.

Which meant that the good sheriff would know exactly who Wyatt was the second he gave his name. Then, in all probability, the entire Ledger clan would likely get word Wyatt was in town before morning.

"I really need to get my car back as soon as possible," Kelly said.

McGuire ran his fingers through his thinning hair. "Yes, ma'am. That's what we're here for. I'll need you to answer a few questions to get us started. It won't take long. If you live around here, you might want to go ahead and call your husband to come pick you up."

"I'm a widow, and I don't have any friends in the area that I can call. I'm in the process of moving to Mustang Run from another part of the country. The moving van is delivering my furniture in the morning."

"Mustang Run. Good place to live," the sheriff said. "Live there myself and have for most of my life. Believe me, you'll have plenty of friends soon. It's that kind of town." He nodded toward Wyatt. "So I take it you two aren't together."

"No," Wyatt said. "I was the only other customer when the car was stolen and I just stayed around to offer a little moral support. I can clear out now if I'm not needed." Before he ran smack into the legend of Troy Ledger. He'd as soon not face that tonight.

"How about hanging around a few more minutes?" the sheriff said. "Brent and I will want to ask you a few questions, as well."

That eliminated the easy escape. But on one level, he was relieved. He was curious about Kelly Burger. And a bit concerned that the thug who had looked at her like he was the wolf and she was the lamb now knew where she lived and had likely overheard Jaci's comment about her father being dead. He might figure she and Jaci would be alone tonight.

The bell over the door tinkled again and this time a burly guy accompanied by a petite blonde walked in. Edie greeted them by name. Judging from the comments, they were a truck-driving team who stopped by often. Edie scurried off to take care of them.

"Is that your Corvette out there?" the sheriff asked Wyatt.

"No. I'm driving the black pickup truck. I figure the guy who stole Ms. Burger's Honda drove up in that. It was the only car parked out front when I came in and he was the only customer."

"A Honda for a Corvette. Interesting trade. Brent, run the plates on the Corvette. My guess is it's hot."

Good assumption. Wyatt sipped his coffee while

the sheriff gathered the basic information from Kelly. His interest piqued when they got to the address where Kelly would be living.

"That's the old Callister place, isn't it?" McGuire asked. "Yellow cottage-style house, down from the old Baptist church."

"Yes. How did you know?"

"My daughter Collette rented the place for a while back when she was single. I was glad to see her move out."

"Why?" Kelly asked.

"I probably shouldn't even mention this," McGuire said, "but I'm sure you'll hear from someone else if not from me. My daughter's friend was brutally attacked in that house. She's fine now, but it was touch-and-go for a while. Turned out the guy was actually after my daughter. But don't worry. He's behind bars now."

"I hope your daughter is okay," Kelly said.

"She's fine now. Married and with a bun in the oven."

Wyatt was familiar with that part of the story. The sheriff's daughter was married to Wyatt's brother Dylan. This was becoming all too familial. All they needed was some fried chicken and banana pudding and it would be a family reunion.

How did people ever have any privacy in a town like Mustang Run?

"That house has been empty for over a year," McGuire continued. "Place needs a paint job and lots of work. Last time I drove by to check things out, I noticed an oak tree in front that needs to be cut down."

"I loved that tree. I remember climbing it when I was about Jaci's age and having tea parties with Grams under those huge spreading branches."

"Well, it's dead now. Lightning bolt last spring nailed it and it looks like the first good wind will lay it on the roof."

"I wasn't made aware of any of that."

"House was in perfect shape when Cordelia Callister was living. She'd probably roll over in her grave if she knew it was in such a state of disrepair."

"Surely it isn't that bad."

"It's bad enough that whoever rented it to you should have explained how much work it needs before they took your money. If you need help breaking the lease, call Judge Betty Smith. Number's in the book. She'll tell you what to do."

"Actually, I own that house," Kelly admitted. "I had no idea it was neglected. For years, I've been paying a man named Arnold Jenkins to manage the property."

McGuire rubbed his whiskered jaw. "So you own the old Callister home place? Did you buy it sight unseen?"

"I didn't buy it. I inherited it. Cordelia was my grandmother."

"Well, hell's bells. Then you must be Linda Ann's daughter. Why didn't you say so?"

"I didn't expect anyone around here to remember my mother."

"All the old-timers around here remember her. She grew up in Mustang Run and that was back when everybody knew everybody."

It appeared they still did.

McGuire hooked his thumbs in his belt loop and hitched up his pants. "Don't that beat all, you showing up back here after all these years? Linda Ann left Mustang Run right after she graduated from UT and that's pretty much the last we've seen of her. How's she doing?"

"Mother's doing well."

"I remember Cordelia talking about Linda Ann being a single mother after your father was killed. Car crash, wasn't it?"

Kelly nodded. "He died before I was born."

McGuire rubbed his jaw. "Did Linda Ann ever marry again?"

"Yes, six years ago. She married a physics professor that she worked with in Boston. He retired last year and surprisingly, they moved to Plano, Texas."

"Guess your grandmother figured Linda Ann wasn't ever going to move back to Mustang Run so she just left her property to you."

"Exactly. But apparently I should have checked on it personally before now. In my defense, I've been occupied with other matters and I trusted that Mr. Jenkins was taking care of repairs."

"I'm afraid Arnold's been snookering you for over a year. He's got the rheumatism so bad now he had to give up his membership in the local spit-and-whittle society. He's been at his son's house in California since before Thanksgiving."

"Spit and whittle?" Kelly questioned, confusion written on her face.

"The unofficial society for retired men," Wyatt explained. And now that he'd interrupted the dialogue, he might as well come clean and jump into the old-home-week party.

Wyatt stuck out a hand toward the sheriff. "I should introduce myself. I'm Wyatt Ledger."

The sheriff's eyebrows rose. He leaned back on his heels, studying Wyatt. "Yep, I see the family resemblance now. Dylan talks about you all the time, but he didn't say a word about his infamous Atlanta detective brother coming for a visit."

"No one in the family knows I'm here," Wyatt admitted.

"Planning to surprise 'em, uh? Believe me, they will be. Sure as shootin', Troy will kill the fatted calf. How long you here for?"

"I'm not sure."

"Well, I'd like to sit down and chew the fat with you while you're in town, see how the big-city way of doing things compares with our methods. The county is growing so fast, we're adding a specialized homicide division. I could use your input."

"I'd be glad to give it."

"Right now we'd better get to the business at hand."

Wyatt caught a whiff of Kelly's perfume as she and the sheriff stepped away. Add that to the sway of her hips and the effect was intoxicating.

A half hour later, it had all been said. As suspected, the Corvette had been stolen in Houston earlier that day, the keys taken from a woman in her own driveway as she was getting in the car.

While the sheriff had questioned Kelly, Brent had taken down a detailed description of the suspect from Wyatt and Edie. Jaci was still sleeping soundly.

McGuire took another call on his cell phone, the third since he'd arrived. Evidently the weather was playing havoc with driving. When the sheriff broke the connection, he gulped down the remains of his second cup of coffee and turned to Wyatt.

"I've got a truck that skidded off the road and into a ditch on Buchanan Road that I need to attend to. Seeing as how both you and Mrs. Burger are going to Mustang Run, how about you giving her a lift into town?"

An offer Wyatt had made earlier and had the proposal refused. But that was when he and Kelly were strangers. Now they shared a membership in the elite Mustang Run descendants club.

Now Wyatt was the one with concerns. "I'll be glad to drive Mrs. Burger into town, but I don't think it's a good idea for her to stay at her house tonight."

"The house needs work, but it's not going to cave in on her," McGuire argued. "It's been standing for more than a hundred years."

"The thief looked about as unsavory as they come," Wyatt said. "Even if he can't break into her computer files, there's information in the stolen car about where she lives. And I suspect he has a good hunch she'll be there alone."

"More likely, the thief is long gone from the area by now," McGuire said. "But the decision for where she stays is up to Mrs. Burger."

Kelly chewed her bottom lip nervously and turned toward Wyatt. "Do you really think Jaci and I might be in danger?"

"Probably not, but why chance it? Spend the night in a motel and give the guy plenty of time to move on. There are two in town."

"That's an option," the sheriff agreed, "but they might not have a vacancy tonight. They're small motels and there's a big gun show in town this weekend."

"It wouldn't hurt to check them out," Wyatt said.

The sheriff pulled a ring of keys from his pocket and rattled them as if he were eager to leave. "Tell you what, if you do stay at the house, I'll have one of the deputies do drive-bys every hour or so. If you get anxious or even think you hear someone trying to break in, call 911 and he can get there quicker than a snake can slither through a hollow log."

Kelly pushed her half bangs away from her face. "I'd appreciate that."

Wyatt still didn't like it, but it seemed he wasn't getting a vote. But as long as he was driving Kelly and Jaci into town, he still had time to talk Kelly into staying in a motel.

He was being overly cautious. But then, dealing with dead victims on a regular basis did that for a man.

McGuire got as far as the door and turned back. "Another option would be to drive Mrs. Burger and her daughter out to Willow Creek Ranch. I'm sure Troy would be glad to put them up for the night," McGuire said. "There's plenty of room in that rambling old house."

Wyatt nodded, but he wasn't keen on that idea.

"You two work it out and let me know what you decide. The deputy can be in the area if you need him, Mrs. Burger. But now that I think about it, staying out at the Ledger ranch is what I'd recommend."

"I'll go make room for a couple of extra passengers in my truck," Wyatt said, deciding to leave before he said too much. As far as he was concerned, the ranch was a last resort. Reuniting with Troy would be stressful enough without pulling a woman he barely knew into the sticky mix.

Fortunately, the rain had stopped, since making room for two passengers required moving his clothes from the backseat to the covered bed of the truck. When the truck was ready, he made one quick call to Alyssa and then went back for his two charges.

The intriguing and naively seductive Kelly Burger would be the first female passenger in his new truck.

This was where Alyssa's ridiculous raised-by-a-family-of-skunks analogy might actually come in handy.

Too bad that Kelly smelled so damn good.

Chapter Four

Miraculously, Jaci barely stirred when Kelly strapped her into the seat belt. Kelly made a support pillow of her lightweight jacket for her daughter.

"I'll turn on some heat," Wyatt said as she settled into the front passenger seat.

"Thanks. Neither Jaci nor I are dressed for this weather. I knew there was a cold front predicted for tonight, but I expected to be in Mustang Run long before now."

"What made you late?"

"Car trouble."

"Tough. That's the kind of luck I'd have wished on the thief."

They grew silent after that and she leaned back, closed her eyes and contemplated Wyatt and the idea of renting a motel room tonight. She'd counted on staying in the empty house, only now the pillows and sleeping bags she'd packed were speeding down the highway with a low-down thief.

The scenario that Wyatt had brought up was far worse. The thief with the stare that had made her skin crawl could be in Mustang Run, waiting for her and Jaci to arrive.

More than likely, he was miles away by now, just as the sheriff had theorized. But what if the sheriff was wrong? She shivered at the possibility.

"I think I will take your advice and stay at the motel tonight," she said. "Even if they catch the thief, it sounds as if there's little chance I'd get my car back right away. And without the sleeping bags, Jaci and I would be sleeping on the cold, hard floor."

"Good. That will save me having to sleep in my truck outside your house. Overnight stakeouts are the devil on a man's back."

"The sheriff offered protection."

"You know the old adage. A cop on the scene is worth two in a roaming patrol car."

"I thought it was a bird in the hand was worth two in the bush."

"Now who would want a bird in his hand?"

She smiled in spite of the tense situation. Wyatt Ledger was definitely nice to have around in a crunch.

"I hope there's somewhere I can rent a car early in the morning," she said.

"I kind of doubt there's a car rental location in Mustang Run, but if there's not, I can always drive you into Austin to pick one up."

"I couldn't ask you to do that. There must be some kind of taxi or car service to the Austin airport. I'm sure the motel will know how to contact them."

"My fares are a lot cheaper."

"I'm sure you have better things to do than chauffeur me around."

"Not particularly. I'm unemployed. I could use the entertainment."

"According to Sheriff McGuire, you'll be dining on a fatted calf."

"That's what I'm afraid of."

"Ah, now I get it. You're looking for an escape valve in case the pressure of family becomes overbearing."

"Darn. You figured me out." He slowed to maneuver around a low spot where water had collected on the road. "Seriously, you're having a run of bad luck, Kelly. It could happen to anyone, but I'd be a jerk not to offer my help and protection."

She'd like to believe that was the total truth and that all his intentions were good, but with what she'd been through the past year, it was hard to trust anyone.

Kelly shifted and stretched, fatigue settling into her shoulders and neck. "How long has it been since you've visited Mustang Run?"

"Nineteen years last September."

"You sound like my mother. She left Mustang Run and except for a few quick visits to check on my grandmother when she was ill, Mother never returned to her hometown."

"I'm sure she had her reasons," Wyatt said.

"If she did, she didn't talk about them other than to say that the town was too small."

"Obviously, you didn't agree with her since you're moving here."

"I'm not sure how long I'll stay. I'm in a regrouping phase of life." She leaned back and let her head drop to the padded rest. "How long has it been since you've seen your father?"

"Eighteen years, give or take a few months."

"There must be a story there."

"Yes, but it's not the kind you tell to impress a woman you've just met."

If he was trying to impress her, he was doing a

bang-up job of it. "Okay, let me guess," she said. "Your family is a notorious gang of bank robbers."

He faked a shocked expression. "You've met them."

"You're lying. Let me see… Second guess," she said, playing along. "Your brothers are secretly vampires in cowboy clothing."

He produced a lecherous smile. "Did anyone ever tell you that you have a lovely neck?"

"All the time," she said. "My earlobes get a lot of attention, too."

"I don't doubt it."

She closed her eyes as the knots in her stomach began to slowly unravel. She refused to let herself dwell on the idea of Wyatt's lips on her neck or any other part of her body, but his easy banter was definitely helping to put things in perspective.

Her car had been stolen. That was nothing compared to what she'd been through over the last twelve months. If she didn't get her car back, she'd collect the insurance and buy another one.

And the pervert who stole it was likely several counties away by now, using her cash to provide his next high.

They passed the Mustang Run city-limits sign, and Kelly turned so that she could check on Jaci, though the rhythmic sounds of her breathing were proof she was still asleep. The doll she carried everywhere was clutched to her chest.

"If I remember right, the house is only a few miles from here," Kelly said. "Could we stop by there on the way to the motel? After the sheriff's diatribe on the condition it's in, I'd just like a little advance warning of what I have to face in the morning."

"Sure. Where do I turn?"

"Wait. I have the address plugged into my phone's GPS system." She looked it up and fed him the directions. In less than five minutes, they turned off on a blacktop road. Two minutes more and they passed the old Baptist church she remembered from the few times she'd visited her grandmother.

"We should be just about there. You'll have to watch for the drive. The house may be hard to see in the dark."

Kelly's hands grew clammy as Wyatt pulled into the driveway. Before her car was stolen, she had been excited about moving into the house. She needed a place with continuity and history and a tie to the grandmother she'd loved but never really gotten to know.

Unlike her mother, Kelly found the idea of a small town appealing, especially at this point in her life. She wanted a quiet, safe town where she could take Jaci to the park and let her play in the yard.

Still, an unreasonable dread tightened her chest as beams of illumination from Wyatt's headlights disbanded the shadows. And then she spied the latest disaster.

Kelly jumped out of the truck the second it stopped and stamped to the steps for a closer look. A huge branch of the oak tree McGuire had mentioned had crashed through the roof of the house.

Chimney bricks and ripped shingles were scattered about the porch and the weed-filled flower bed. Turning away, she was lashed at by a gust of wind that whipped her hair into her eyes and mouth.

She kicked at a pile of shingles and then jumped back with a squeal when a giant tarantula crawled away from the debris.

"The spider's harmless," Wyatt said.

"That doesn't mean I have to like him."

Kelly clenched her teeth and tried to calm her wrath. She had little success, but she did lower her voice so that she wouldn't wake Jaci.

"I was prepared for a few loose shutters and peeling paint, not a hole in my roof that a helicopter could fly through."

That was a slight exaggeration, but nonetheless the house was totally unlivable. And she had a van full of furniture that had been in storage for a year arriving in the morning.

"How can anyone have the kind of luck I've had today?" Her words were clipped. Her insides were positively shaking.

"I'd say you've had at least one stroke of good luck."

"I must have blinked during that stroke."

"That car trouble that delayed you may have saved you and Jaci from serious injury when that tree fell."

She hadn't thought of that. It did little to ease her frustration.

"I can get my flashlight from the truck and check out the damage inside, but you won't be able to determine the full extent of the destruction until daylight."

"Don't bother with checking the damage. I've seen enough of the house and Mustang Run. I'd just get in my car and keep driving, except that I don't have a car."

Her voice broke and her eyes burned with salty tears. One escaped from the corner of her right eye and she brushed it away with the back of her hand. She'd lived though a year of hell, without once allowing herself to whimper or go berserk. She wouldn't break now. She was stronger than that.

Wyatt stepped closer and slipped an arm around her shoulder. "It's not the end of the world," he said. "It just seems like it."

"Don't be nice," she said. "I can't take nice." The tears started to flow and she couldn't stop them.

She didn't say a word. Neither did Wyatt. He just held her until her insides stopped shaking and the tears ran dry.

"I'm not usually like this," she said, finally pulling away.

"Good. I'd hate to have to wear a bib every time we were together to keep my shirts dry."

As usual, he kept the moment light. No doubt he didn't want her to read too much into his supplying broad shoulders for her to cry on. Kelly backed away from the mortally wounded house. "Let's get out of here. Just drop me off at the motel and you can escape before the black cloud over me sucks you into its vacuity too."

"Actually I won't be dropping you off. I'll be staying." She bristled and the air rushed from her lungs. If he thought holding her while she cried entitled him to—

"Not in your room," he said quickly, before she had the chance to make a fool of herself. "And before you get all bent out of shape, my decision to stay at the motel has nothing to do with you."

"Then what does it have to do with?"

"If I go barging in on my father unexpectedly this time of night, it's likely that neither he nor I will get any sleep."

"Okay, if you're sure. But don't stay on my account. I'm okay now. Really."

"I believe you. But since I'll be at the motel anyway, I may as well drive you wherever you need to go in the morning. Without strings, in case you're worried about that."

No wonder so many women loved cowboys.

Not that she had any intention of falling for Wyatt Ledger. He should be happy to hear that. It might save him from contracting the plague.

In fact, there was no real reason for her and Jaci to even stay in Mustang Run now. The anticipated roof over their heads had literally collapsed.

No vacancy.

The news was no better at the second motel they visited than it had been at the first. Considering the number of cars in the lot, Wyatt wasn't surprised.

"I wish we could help you out," the young clerk said, "but every room in the motel has been booked for months."

"You must have at least one no-show," Kelly insisted, a trace of desperation in her voice.

"Actually we had three last-minute cancellations, but we had a waiting list for the rooms."

"And all of this is for a gun show?" Wyatt asked.

The clerk nodded. "Happens every January. It's kind of a male-bonding ritual, like tailgating at the Longhorn games and drinking beer at fishing tournaments."

"There must be gun shows in Austin," Wyatt said. "What makes this one so special?"

"All the major manufacturers take part in it. And it's not just looking at the latest models. You get to handle the weapons and even shoot them for a small fee. There's shooting contests and they even have a wild-game cook-off tomorrow out in the parking lot of the town hall. Big prizes and good eating."

Jaci drowsily released her grip on her mother's waist and sat down on the floor.

Kelly stooped and picked her up, balancing the child on her right hip.

"Do you want me to hold her?" Wyatt asked.

Jaci tightened her grip around her mother's neck.

"Thanks, but she's not that heavy."

He breathed easier. Not that he minded the weight, but he hadn't been around kids much. He'd done all right with Jaci's crying mother, but no sense to push his luck.

The kid had woken just as they'd pulled into the parking lot, and Kelly had jumped at the chance for her and Jaci to come in with him. He figured she wasn't convinced he'd pleaded his case well enough at the motel across the highway.

"That significantly cuts down on our options," Wyatt said.

Kelly reached in her pocket and retrieved her phone as they left the motel and stepped back into the cold, damp air. "You have an option, Wyatt. You have family in town. I'm the one with the problem."

"So you're suggesting I just dump you and Jaci on the street and then go crawl into a warm bed?"

"I'm calling for a taxi to drive us to the nearest hotel, motel, B and B, dude ranch or any other establishment that actually has an available room for rent. I'm not too picky at this point."

"No telling what kind of dump you'd end up at."

"Fine by me, as long as it's a dump with a bed."

"Get in the truck, Kelly. You're tired. I'm tired. Jaci's exhausted. Willow Creek Ranch has plenty of beds and a roof."

He opened the door to the backseat so that she could buckle Jaci in.

"You've done more than enough—"

"Yeah, I know. I'm Mr. Wonderful."

"We should at least call your father and ask if he's okay with this," she said, obviously giving in.

"No need. He'll be thrilled. Troy's Mr. Wonderful, Senior. If you run into any of my brothers or sisters-in-law, they'll all assure you of that."

Kelly kissed Jaci on the top of her sleepy blond head and closed the back door. "You don't sound convinced of that fact."

"That's why I'm back in Mustang Run, so he can convince me. But don't worry. He's not an ogre. And unlike me, he's good with kids. He has two grandchildren. They love him and he practically worships them."

"I still think you should call him first."

"You heard the sheriff. The door to Troy Ledger's house is always open to family and friends."

Kelly didn't wince at the mention of Troy Ledger, which meant she had no idea who he was. But then according to the sheriff, Kelly's mother had moved out of Mustang Run before Kelly was born and that would have been well before the murder. Wyatt had been thirteen at the time, the oldest of all of Troy's sons.

"I guess I should call Sheriff McGuire and let him know I won't need his deputy to check on me tonight."

She made the call, filling McGuire in on the half of a tree that had crashed through her roof. After that, she leaned back and closed her eyes, leaving Wyatt to drive the rest of the way to the ranch with nothing but his own disturbing thoughts for entertainment.

There were times lately when he'd talked to Dylan, Sean or Dakota that he could almost believe that Troy was the same loving father he'd been when they were brats running wild and free around the ranch and not the hot-tempered, jealous monster his mother's family had brainwashed him to believe he was.

But Wyatt was a homicide detective. He knew how often the husband of the victim was painted in glowing terms by his kids before the perverted truth came out.

Wyatt hoped to God he'd find out his father was innocent—but either way, he had to know the truth.

Images flooded Wyatt's mind like the murky waters of a muddied bayou as he got out of the truck to open the gate to Willow Creek Ranch. His mother's body stretched across the floor, covered by a sheet someone had ripped from her bed. Blood pooled beneath her, smeared across her face, matted in her beautiful long, dark hair.

His mother. Always there when he needed her. Always smiling. She danced and sang around the house, was generous with hugs, but not a pushover for her sons' mischievous misadventures.

Helene Ledger. As steady as a sunrise. As comforting as moonbeams. She was the perfect mom.

But Troy had been his hero.

He'd lost them both that day.

He felt Kelly's eyes on him as he braked in front of the rambling ranch house.

"You look upset, Wyatt. What's wrong?"

"Nothing."

"Your mood has grown steadily darker ever since you drove through the gate. If you didn't want to bring me here, why did you?"

"My mood has nothing to do with you. But I admit there are unresolved issues between me and my father."

"What kind of issues, or is that none of my business?"

"You'll hear about my father sooner or later anyway, so I guess you may as well hear it from me. First, make sure Jaci is fast asleep. This is not a fit discussion for young ears."

Kelly shifted for a view of the backseat. "Out like a light. So what is it with you and your father?"

"Eighteen years ago he was convicted of murder one and sentenced to life."

"Oh, no."

"It gets worse. The victim was Helene Ledger, my mother."

"Oh, Wyatt. That's so sad. You must have been just a kid. But surely they found out that he was innocent or he'd still be in prison."

"He was released approximately a year and a half ago on a technicality."

"But Sheriff McGuire must believe he's innocent or he wouldn't have suggested you bring me and Jaci to the ranch."

"He may be convinced of Troy's innocence now, but Sheriff McGuire conducted the investigation that led to my father's arrest. But don't worry. I wouldn't have brought you and Jaci here if there was any chance that you'd be in danger. If Troy's guilty, Mom's murder was the only unprovoked violence ever attributed to him."

"Did he confess to the crime?"

"No, he's proclaimed his innocence since day one. And, according to my brothers, he spends every minute he's not working the ranch searching for my mother's killer or at least researching suspects."

As Wyatt turned off the ignition and switched off the high beams, the porch light flicked on and Troy Ledger stepped onto the porch.

Wyatt had waited eighteen years for this meeting. And yet as he climbed out of the truck, his legs felt like solid lead.

Chapter Five

Troy stared at the couple making their way up the short walkway from the driveway toward his house. The woman was holding a sleeping preschooler. The child was petite, but still you'd think the man would be carrying her since his hands were empty.

The woman stared at him, uncertainty in her step and plastered on her face, as if she wasn't sure they were at the right place.

He suspected they weren't. He wasn't expecting company, especially not at almost ten o'clock on a stormy night. The woman was attractive, but her shoulders drooped as if she were exhausted.

He turned his attention to the man. Tall. Nice Stetson. A swagger to his walk that suggested he knew exactly where he was. Recognition flickered and then rushed through Troy's veins like an injection of pure adrenaline.

His last son had come home.

Troy hurried down the steps to meet him, but once they were eye to eye, Troy's mouth went dry and he had to force the name from his mouth.

"Wyatt."

"Yep, it's me." Wyatt stuck out a hand in greeting.

Troy ignored it and flung an arm about his son's shoulder. He'd been through this with every other son, the painful silences and numerous obstacles to overcome while they were getting to know each other all over again.

But this was Wyatt, his firstborn. He still remembered his beautiful Helene laying Wyatt in his arms that first time. The responsibility of fatherhood had hung over Troy like a dead weight before that moment. But once he'd held Wyatt in his arms, he knew that he'd move heaven and earth to keep Helene and Wyatt happy and safe.

He'd failed them both.

"Why didn't you call and let me know you were coming?" Troy asked.

"I took my time driving over from Atlanta so I wasn't sure when I'd get here."

"You're here now. That's all that matters. Have you talked to your brothers?"

"Not lately. I figured I'd surprise them, too. I'll see Dylan and Dakota tomorrow since they're here at the ranch. I'll give Sean a call and try to catch up with him sometime this weekend."

"Good thinking. If you call them tonight, Dylan and Dakota will be here before you climb out of bed in the morning. It won't take Sean much longer."

Jaci squirmed and opened her eyes.

"I'm sorry," Troy said, turning to Kelly. "I was so excited over seeing Wyatt, I forgot my manners. I'm Troy Ledger."

"I'm Kelly Burger and this is my daughter, Jaci. I feel bad about intruding this way, but all the motels in town are full and Wyatt said you wouldn't mind putting us up for the night."

"Of course I don't mind. Any friend of Troy's is welcome anytime. Let's get you and Jaci out of the cold and then we'll do proper introductions."

"Good idea," Wyatt agreed.

"Wyatt, why don't you grab Kelly's bags out of the car while I show them inside, in case she wants to get Jaci settled in for the night."

"I don't have luggage," Kelly said, "but I'm sure Jaci will appreciate a bed."

Jaci balled her hands into fists and rubbed her eyes. "Are we home, Momma?"

"No, sweetheart, but we're going to stay with these nice people tonight."

Jaci looked around and then laid her head back on her mother's shoulder. "The bad man took our car."

"I'll explain it all inside," Wyatt said.

Troy led the way, pushing the door open and then standing back for Kelly to step inside.

"I hope we didn't wake you," she said.

"No, I just got back from the horse barn. A couple of the fillies get jittery during storms. If no one's there to calm them, they can get the other horses riled. Normally my daughter-in-law Collette would insist on being down there with them. But she's eight months pregnant now."

Jaci's eyes opened wider. "Where are the horses?"

Kelly brushed curly wisps of hair back from Jaci's face. "They're in the barn asleep."

"Why don't I go ahead and show you to your rooms?" Troy said. "Then you can get Jaci settled whenever you want."

Kelly switched Jaci to her other hip. "I'd appreciate that."

Wyatt didn't follow them down the hallway.

"There are several bedrooms, so you can spread out as much as you like," he offered, not sure exactly what kind of relationship Kelly and Wyatt shared.

"I'd prefer Jaci sleep in the room with me," Kelly answered quickly. "It's been a long, hard day for both of us and I think she'd feel more secure if I'm nearby."

"The guest room off the garden is the most roomy and comfortable choice. It has a queen-size bed but there's a room with two twins if you prefer."

"The garden room sounds perfect. I'm so tired tonight that I could probably sleep on the ground."

"Too cold for that tonight. They're forecasting freezing temperatures."

He pointed out the bathroom and the closet that held extra blankets and pillows if she needed them and then opened the door to the guest suite that Helene had created. She'd combed garage sales and auctions for over a year looking for affordable antiques. Then she'd spent hours refinishing them.

"It's a beautiful room," Kelly said.

"I hope it's comfortable for you."

"I'm sure it will be."

By the time he got back to the kitchen, Wyatt was on his cell phone, pacing the kitchen and doing more listening than talking.

Troy didn't intentionally eavesdrop as he pulled a couple of beers from the fridge, but there was no missing the troubled tone or the gist of what he overheard.

The discussion concerned Kelly Burger and Wyatt clearly didn't like what he was hearing.

Troy opened his beer and downed half of it while Wyatt finished the conversation.

"Care for a beer, or do you need something stronger?" he offered once Wyatt broke the connection.

Wyatt dropped into a chair at the kitchen table. "A beer would be great."

"Problems?" Troy asked as he sat down opposite Wyatt and pushed the longneck bottle across the table.

"Complications. Nothing I can't deal with."

"Is this strictly a friendly visit to Mustang Run or are you in the area on police business?"

"Strictly personal—at least at this point."

Troy wasn't sure what to make of that comment. "I'm glad you're here no matter the reason, Wyatt. Really glad."

"You already have four sons practically in your hip pocket."

Troy didn't miss the hint of sarcasm. He understood where it was coming from. "Your brothers had reservations when they first came back to the ranch, same as I'm sure you have. We worked through them—once they met me halfway."

Now Dylan and Dakota were living on the ranch with their wives. Sean and his wife and stepson, Joey, just lived over in Bandera. And Travis would return from Afghanistan in a matter of months.

Wyatt looked around the kitchen before making eye contact with Troy. "We have good reason for reservations."

"No one knows that better than me," Troy said. "I've made a lot of mistakes. I should have never accepted your grandparents' insistence that none of you wanted anything to do with me."

"Can't undo what's been done," Wyatt said.

"No, but we can move on from here. You're part of this family, a big part. Every one of your brothers has gone to you for advice at one time or another over the last year and a half."

"Doing what's right now doesn't make up for letting them down years ago."

"Are we still talking about you, because as far as I know, you never failed anyone."

"It doesn't matter. You're absolutely right, Troy. I'm here because I'm a Ledger."

Troy. As if Wyatt wasn't his son. It hurt, but he could understand his reluctance to call him dad.

"Hopefully you'll get to stay long enough that we can hash out the past and get to a better place," Troy said.

"That would be good."

"For all of us. And sometime while you're here, I'd like to pick your brain."

"About what?"

"My investigation into your mother's murder. I've spent hours trying to put my finger on a viable suspect, but every time I think I'm making progress, I run up against a brick wall. The clues are like a math problem where the numbers change before I can solve the equation."

Wyatt straightened in his chair and turned to stare out the kitchen window. "I promise that I'll make time to look at everything you've discovered."

The assurance sounded sincere, but Wyatt still seemed distracted. Troy had a good hunch that Kelly Burger and her stolen car had something to do with that.

"Kelly and her daughter seem nice," Troy baited. "Have you known her long?"

"About four hours." Wyatt took another sip of beer and then rocked the bottom of the bottle on the wooden table. "Kelly and I met earlier this evening at a truck stop café about forty miles from here. We'd both gone in to escape the worst of the storm."

"Smart move."

"It turned out to be an unfortunate move for Kelly."

"How's that?"

"There was just one other customer in the café," Wyatt continued. "He left in the middle of the storm. About a half hour later when the rain had almost stopped, Kelly went outside and discovered the bastard had stolen her car. The vehicle he left in its place was stolen, as well."

"You were right to bring them here," Troy said after Wyatt explained about the problems with Kelly's house and with finding a room. "They can stay as long as they like, unless you have a problem with their being here. They won't bother me and there's plenty of room."

"It works for me, but I'm not sure Kelly will take you up on the offer. She's spunky as hell and independent to a fault. But I figure I can at least help her get that tree off the house so that she can get an accurate estimate of the damage."

"Does she have insurance?" Troy asked.

"I'm assuming she does. We didn't talk about it." Wyatt finished his beer. "There's a lot we didn't discuss. But we will."

There was that edge again.

"Is there anything else about Kelly I should know?" Troy asked.

"You know as much about her as I do."

Troy suspected that wasn't quite the full truth. "She looked exhausted," Troy said. "I wouldn't be surprised if she's already asleep, but in case she isn't, there's a fully stocked basket of guest toiletries on the top shelf of the hall closet. And there's ham, cheese, bread and condiments if she wants a sandwich."

"I'll let her know."

"Are you hungry?"

"No. I had a burger earlier."

"Be sure and tell Kelly that there's milk for Jaci. Skim milk, however. That's all the doc lets me drink since my heart attack."

"Dylan tells me that you're back to doing almost everything on the ranch that you were doing before the attack."

"So far, so good."

"Good to hear." Wyatt pushed back from the table. "It's been a long day for me, too. We can talk more tomorrow, but I need to hit the sack now. Any bed will do."

"Kelly and Jaci are in the guest room that opens to the garden, but your old bedroom is available. There are clean sheets on the bed and fresh towels in all the bathrooms."

"Sounds as if you were expecting company."

"No, but Collette talked me into hiring a housekeeper. She was afraid that with all the work Dylan, Dakota and I have been putting in on the ranch, I'd let the house slide into a state of utter chaos."

Wyatt stood and looked around the spacious kitchen again. "Housekeeper must be working out. Things look good."

"Wait until you see the ranch."

"We'll make plans for the five-dollar tour after breakfast," Wyatt said. "What time is breakfast around here or is it every man for himself?"

"I'll be up with the sun. You'll smell the coffee and

hear the sizzle of turkey bacon shortly thereafter. But feel free to sleep as late as you like."

"Thanks. I probably won't be eating on the early-bird shift. I haven't had a lot of sleep the last couple of nights."

Wyatt stood, sauntered to the refrigerator and retrieved a second beer before walking away. Troy was tired himself but knew that sleep might be a long time in coming tonight.

Wyatt's homecoming was strained. That didn't surprise him. Too many years had passed, years when Troy had existed as the imprisoned killer whose blood ran through his sons' veins. Helene's parents had made sure that was all any of his sons knew of Troy, and he'd done nothing to convince them otherwise.

Troy spotted Wyatt standing near the hearth to the huge stone fireplace, staring at the spot where Helene's body had been found. His jaw was clenched. His face was stretched into hard, drawn lines.

Troy knew all too well the images that must be running roughshod through his mind.

For Troy, having to walk by that spot every day had been the most difficult part of returning to the ranch. Even now, the images were so real at times that Troy would break out in a cold sweat.

Troy ached to walk over and put an arm around Wyatt's shoulder, tell him that he knew his young heart had been brutally ripped apart the day she'd been killed. He'd like to apologize for failing Wyatt and all his brothers in the days and months following Helene's tragic death.

But words were meaningless. Like his four other sons, Wyatt would make peace with the past in his own way, in his own time. At least Troy prayed that he would.

That peace had never come for Troy. It wouldn't until he found the man who'd killed Helene and stolen all their lives.

THE GUEST ROOM WAS positively enchanting. Kelly felt as if she'd been dropped into the early nineteenth century, complete with the most charming bedside lamp she'd ever seen. The shade was handpainted with exquisite ruby-red roses. The frame was cast iron.

A similar lamp sat atop a carved mahogany antique dresser with a beveled mirror. The four-poster bed was in the same rich wood. Having spent countless hours scouring New Orleans antique shops before Jaci was born, Kelly could tell that the bed was an original antique that had been restored and meticulously extended in size.

Someone had spent many hours designing and furnishing this cozy sanctuary. She wondered if it had been Wyatt's mother. If so, Kelly would love to know more about her.

Had she been quiet and loving or filled with exuberance for life? Had she been happy here? Or had she longed to escape? Had she loved her husband? Had she feared him?

Had he killed her?

Coming home after nineteen years to the place where he'd known joy and such heartbreaking loss must be traumatic for Wyatt. And yet he'd kept that all inside, not showing the first signs of apprehension until he'd driven through the Willow Creek Ranch gate.

Yet with all that on his mind, he'd come to her rescue as if it were the most natural thing in the world to offer protection to a desperate woman and kid he'd never seen before.

He'd been calm and steady, keeping his own feelings locked away inside while she'd had a meltdown. No wonder he'd offered to bring her home with him. He probably thought her incapable of taking care of herself or Jaci.

Now she would be sleeping in the home of a man who'd been convicted of murdering his wife. She should be extremely wary. For some weird reason, she wasn't. Instead, Troy had made her feel at ease and welcome, almost like family.

Kelly considered the irony of that as she walked to the room's double glass doors. The curtains were already pushed back, letting in a glimmer of light through the fogged-over glass.

She released the latch and opened the door. A blast of icy wind slapped her in the face. She closed it quickly, and then used the palm of her hand to clear the condensation.

She was rewarded by an amazing view. A large courtyard garden overflowing with lush plants interspersed with jewel-toned pansies, white narcissus and a couple of other winter blooming varieties she didn't recognize. A lighted fountain provided a shimmery glow to the garden and tiny solar lights snuggled in the creeping ground cover along an uneven stone pathway.

Enthralled in the peaceful beauty, Kelly was startled by a sudden chilly draft and the sensation that she and Jaci were not alone in the room. She spun around, expecting to see Troy or Wyatt at the door.

But only Jaci was in the room and she was sound asleep, snuggled beneath the crisp white sheet and a hand-stitched blue-and-white quilt. Perhaps Kelly was a bit more apprehensive than she'd realized.

The disturbing sensation passed and Kelly dropped to the side of the bed. The irritation with the car theft swelled again. She didn't have so much as a toothbrush with her. Nothing to sleep in. No clean undies.

Worst of all, Jaci's favorite toys and books were in the missing car, leaving her with little familiar comforts to cling to during yet another period of upheaval. Thankfully, she'd dragged her favorite nearly bald doll into the café with her. Jaci would have been devastated had she lost that.

Leaning back, Kelly kicked out of her shoes, pulled her feet onto the bed and let her head fall to the pillow. She'd get up, go to the bathroom and wash up in a few minutes. Tomorrow…

She jerked to a sitting position at the sound of a light tapping on the door. It took a few bewildering seconds to realize where she was and that she'd fallen asleep with all her clothes on.

She checked her watch for the time. Ten past eleven. She'd slept only a few minutes, though she was so out of it she could have easily slept through the night, clothes and all.

Finger taming her hair, she hurried to open the door before whoever was there tapped again and woke up Jaci.

"Did I wake you?" Wyatt asked, keeping his voice low.

"I must have dozed off," she whispered. "But Jaci hasn't stirred since her head hit the pillow."

"I thought you might need these."

He handed her a basket stuffed with an assortment of items. Two new toothbrushes. Individual soaps, lotions, mouthwash and other hotel-size toiletries. There was even a mini folding plastic hairbrush, still in its cellophane wrap.

She leaned against the door. "This is exactly what I need."

"Troy says there's toothpaste in the bathroom, and there's beer, milk and makings for sandwiches in the kitchen. Help yourself."

"Thanks."

"This is worn, but clean," he said, handing her one of his cotton T-shirts that he'd had hanging over his arm. "We can shop for anything else you need after breakfast."

"You and Troy run one terrific homeless shelter, cowboy. Keep this up, and I'll hate leaving. But I will be leaving in the morning, you know."

"What's the hurry? You have nowhere to go. You left your life behind you a year ago."

Her heart plunged. Wyatt had done his homework. In a way she was relieved to have the truth out in the open. She was also irritated that he'd had her checked out so quickly by his police cronies.

"That didn't take long," she whispered to keep from waking Jaci. "You're obviously a good cop."

"Damn good. We need to talk."

Chapter Six

Wyatt had debated with himself whether he should put this conversation off until morning. They'd both be rested then. He'd have had more time to think through the implications of getting involved in Kelly's problems when she obviously didn't want his help.

But Jaci and Troy would be awake then and who knew what family might show up? This might be their best chance for privacy.

Kelly stepped into the hall, pulling the bedroom door shut behind her. "I don't want to wake Jaci."

"We can talk in the kitchen," Wyatt said. "Troy's already gone to bed."

Decades-old floorboards groaned beneath their steps as they maneuvered the dimly lit hallway that Wyatt had used as a raceway for his miniature cars and trucks a lifetime ago. Once, he and Sean had even brought toads inside the house to see which one could get from one end of the hallway to the other the fastest.

His mother had stepped out of Dakota's room with a load of laundry just as the toads reached the door. One of the toads had jumped on her foot and the laundry had gone flying, entangling the other toad in a pillowcase.

Wyatt and Sean had doubled over in laughter. And

then they and their toads had been ushered into the yard. But he'd overheard his parents laughing that night about the toad race.

Wyatt had innocently expected the good times to go on forever, expected to be protected from evil and heartbreak. The same way Josh Whiting had expected that. The same way the cute little girl in the bed down the hall expected that.

Kelly dropped into one of the kitchen chairs. "I guess this is as good a place as any for you to interrogate me."

"This isn't an interrogation."

"It sure feels that way."

"Then I'm handling it wrong."

Kelly rolled her eyes. "Don't worry about the finesse. Let's just get this over with."

"What prompted you to move to Mustang Run?"

"I inherited a house."

"Ten years ago."

Kelly locked her gaze with his. "I don't like this game, Wyatt. What is it you heard about me?"

"That you dropped off the face of the earth a little over a year ago and only recently resurfaced. That your last known employment was with a jewelry store that served as a money laundering front for Emanuel Leaky's smuggling operations."

"And I'm sure you know the details of Emanuel's conviction."

"Couldn't turn on cable news, pick up a newspaper or turn on your computer without hearing about that trial," Wyatt admitted. "I don't remember hearing your name mentioned, though."

Kelly's thumb absently traced the edge of the table.

"So now you wonder which side of the equation I was on."

"That's about it," Wyatt admitted. "Knowing which way to watch for flying bullets is the best way I know to keep from getting blindsided."

"I'd like a glass of water," she said.

"You can have something stronger if you like."

"No, just water. I can get it."

She was up before Wyatt had a chance to push back from the table. He watched the sway of her narrow hips as she walked to the cabinet, pulled out a glass and filled it with cool water from the faucet. A wave of guilt washed over him. He'd invited her here for a respite. Now he was treating her like a suspect in one of his cases.

This might seem like an interrogation to her, but it was starting to feel like harassment to him, and he was the one dishing it out. But he didn't know a better way to get to the truth. If she was in danger, he couldn't just stand by and let her and Jaci face it alone.

Kelly sat down again, a glass of water in hand, the condensation wetting her fingertips. "My involvement in this case is confidential, Wyatt. I was told—no, *ordered*—by the FBI not to talk about it with anyone outside the Bureau. I can't imagine how you obtained your information so quickly."

"Were you in witness protection?"

She nodded.

"Yet you didn't testify at the trial," Wyatt said, trying to get his mind around the facts, or at least around Kelly's version of the story.

Kelly stopped hugging her water glass and used both hands to rake shiny locks of hair from her face. "Why is any of this important to you, Wyatt? All you have to do is drive me back into town tomorrow morning and then I'm out of your life for good."

Out of his life, but not necessarily out of danger. Squealing on Emanuel Leaky would be equated by most people to having a death wish. And if she'd provided any information that led to his conviction, she was likely on a hit list.

"You may find this hard to believe coming from an ex-cop, Kelly, but I'm not trying to establish any wrongdoing on your part. If it were there, the FBI would have found it and you'd be in jail. I'm just trying to assure myself that I'm not tossing you and Jaci to the wolves when I drive you into town tomorrow."

She took another sip of water and then spread her hands out flat on the table. "This can't go any further than this table, Wyatt. You have to promise me that."

"You have my word on that. Unless I find out you're in danger. Then all bets are off."

"Can I depend on that?"

"Scout's honor."

"Were you a Boy Scout?"

"No, but I can tie knots," he said, trying to lighten the mood and end her hesitancy. He turned to check out a scraping sound, but it was just the wind whipping the branches of a tree against the metal gutters.

"How did you get involved with Leaky?" Wyatt asked.

"I didn't know he owned the jewelry shop at the time I took the job. Luther Bonner interviewed and hired me."

And Luther Bonner had later turned state's witness to save his own ass. Bets were on as to how long it would be before one of Emanuel's paid assassins took him out. Even from prison, Emanuel wielded a large sphere of influence in the criminal world.

"Did you work solely at the New Orleans location?" Wyatt asked.

"Yes, I wasn't aware of the other money laundering operations until after I started talking to the FBI. The shop where I was employed specialized in expensive one-of-a-kind jewelry items. The customer base was small but extremely wealthy."

"Were you a clerk?"

"I'm a jewelry designer with a flair for the unusual. I designed everything from diamond tiaras to earrings in the shapes of crabs and fleurs-de-lis."

"Do you have any idea how they decided on you for the job?"

"I had a booth at Jazz Fest. Luther saw my work and seemed impressed."

"How did you finally meet Emanuel?"

"He came into the shop four weeks after I started working there. He introduced himself as Van O'Neil and told me what a great job I was doing. I hadn't realized that the name was one of many aliases. Nor did I realize that Luther's name was only an alias, but after working with him for two years, I still think of him as Luther Bonner."

"What happened after Emanuel introduced himself?"

"He and Luther disappeared behind closed doors for a few hours. Emanuel was there off and on for the next three days. He spent most of that time in the back office conducting business with people I'd never seen in the shop before. That was the pattern throughout the two years I worked there. Fly in for a few days, meet with what I thought were business cronies and then fly out again."

"That didn't make you suspicious?"

"A little. I asked Luther about him. He said Van had other business responsibilities and that he left the running of the jewelry store to him. He made it clear that what Van O'Neil did was none of my business and that I should never confront him."

"So you let it go at that?"

"Don't sound so condescending, Wyatt. I liked my job. It paid well and I had a daughter to support. So, yes. I let it go at that."

"Sorry. I didn't mean to come across as a jerk. I'm just trying to get a handle on this. What finally happened to change the status quo?"

"I came back to the shop one night after dinner to put the finishing touches on a diamond-and-ruby necklace that had to be ready for the Queen of Rex the next morning. Emanuel didn't hear me come in. I overheard a heated argument between him and someone whose voice I didn't recognize."

"What were they arguing about?"

"Emanuel was complaining that his last supply of diamonds had been inferior. The other man accused him of lying and demanded immediate delivery of his order. He had a plane waiting at the airport and assurance that there would be no border patrol interference. I sneaked out without their knowing I'd been there."

And if she hadn't and they'd thought she'd overheard, she'd be dead now and Jaci would be an orphan. That was the way Emanuel worked.

"Did you go to the local police or directly to the FBI?"

"To the FBI since Emanuel and this guy were obviously smuggling something across the border."

"Did they arrest Leaky that night?"

"No, but they intercepted the outgoing plane and discovered a cache of automatic weapons."

"Did Emanuel suspect you tipped them off?"

"No, I continued to work for him for another six months while the FBI conducted the investigation that resulted in the arrest of both Emanuel and Luther on charges of smuggling diamonds into the country from Africa and smuggling illegal arms out of the country to Mexican drug cartels."

Wyatt reconstructed the picture in his mind from what he knew of the trial, what he'd heard earlier tonight and what he'd just heard from Kelly. There were still a few gaping holes.

"Why did the FBI decide not to use you as a witness?"

"After Luther cooperated with them, they didn't think they needed me to get a conviction."

"But still, they kept you protected until after the trial?"

"I was their ace in the hole in case any other part of the case fell through. Since they didn't make me testify, Emanuel has no way of knowing that I was the one who originally blew the whistle on him."

"He could find out you were in witness protection as easily as I did. You disappeared without a paper trail."

"But the FBI intentionally leaked information to Luther early on that I didn't know jack about the operation and that I was an unfriendly witness. They were sure that went directly back to Emanuel."

So all the bases were covered. Hopefully the FBI had that right.

"So when the trial was over and Emanuel Leaky was sentenced, you were dropped from protection?"

"Yes. That's when I decided to move back to Mustang Run. The house Grams had left me is sitting empty so I don't have to worry about rent while I get my career reestablished. So, in spite of my complete meltdown earlier, I'm really not homeless or helpless, Wyatt.

"Well, I might be temporarily homeless, but I'll look for another place to rent tomorrow. And I'm not in danger. I just had my car stolen. It happens to people every day."

Wyatt still had reservations about the danger aspect, but he was a naturally suspicious kind of guy. It went with the territory he roamed.

But admittedly it would be difficult to think she was any more than a random victim today considering that the thief was in the truck stop before she arrived. He'd have had no way of knowing she would stop there.

Only now the thief had her computer. "Was there anything in your computer that could tie you to Emanuel?"

"Absolutely not. The computer is brand-new and I was thoroughly indoctrinated by the FBI on what not to post in any internet medium."

Kelly stretched her arms over her head, making her nipples aim at him like bullets. He clenched his fists and ignored a stirring in another part of his body.

What the hell was wrong with him that he kept reacting to Kelly as if he hadn't been with a woman in months? Oh, yeah. He hadn't.

Still, he was around women all the time at the station. No one else had turned him on like this.

Maybe his protective instincts were getting confused with his libido.

"So now you have the rest of the story," Kelly said. "And confession must be good for the appetite as well as the soul. Suddenly, I'm starving."

"Yeah, me too," Wyatt admitted. He opened the refrigerator and began checking out options.

Kelly checked the pantry. "I found some syrup and a box of pancake mix." She read the directions. "All we need are an egg and some milk and we're in business."

"Eggs… Check. Milk… Check." Wyatt opened the fresh-meat drawer. "And pork sausage and turkey and regular bacon. I suspect the pork is for guests, since Troy had a heart attack a year ago."

With the discussion changed from crime to food, the mood instantly lifted. Wyatt located a square grill and a round, flat griddle. He set them both on top of the range, setting the heat to low under the grill.

He started forming sausage patties, but his gaze kept shifting from the meat to Kelly. He liked her hair. It was shiny and touchable, as if it were waiting for his fingers to tangle with the loose curls. He was captivated by the cute tilt of her nose and her full lips without a trace of makeup. He loved that her shirt brushed her nipples, giving just a hint of the perky mounds waiting to be discovered.

Discovered, but not by him.

At least not anytime soon.

He was here on a mission, and he wouldn't let anything interfere with that. Being back in this house with Troy made the need to find the truth about his mother's murder more pressing than ever. His mother deserved that and if Troy was innocent, he deserved it, too.

Still, as the kitchen filled with sizzling sounds and tantalizing odors, Wyatt couldn't help but think about how long it had been since he'd shared a kitchen with a woman. And never with one who was as tantalizingly tempting as Kelly.

He reached around her to get a spatula for the sausage. She turned at the same time. Her face ended up mere inches from his.

Desire flamed, hot and instant. He took a deep breath and managed to move away without giving in to the lure of her seductive lips.

Think skunks, old boy. Think skunks.

FULL AND SATISFIED, at least as far as her stomach was concerned, Kelly kicked off her shoes and started the water running in the old claw-foot tub. Normally, she would have had a quick shower, but the nagging ache in muscles that had been tense for too long, the deep tub and the convenient bottle of inviting bubble bath made a soak a temptation she couldn't resist.

Her resolve to keep everything secret about her connection with Emanuel Leaky had quickly gone astray. She should have known that hooking up on any level with a cop would backfire.

Yet, she felt an unexpected sense of relief now that she'd finally talked about it with someone outside the FBI. She was more relaxed this minute than she had been in weeks.

Unfortunately, her problems would all be waiting for her when she woke up in the morning. No car. No house. And no Wyatt once she left the Willow Creek Ranch.

She checked her reflection in the mirror as she wiggled out of her jeans. It was positively not her best night in the looks department. And yet Wyatt had come within a heartbeat of kissing her while they were cooking. He'd backed off quickly enough, but there was no denying the heat that had passed between them.

Kelly finished undressing, pausing to study her breasts in the narrow mirror as the bra fell to the floor. They weren't huge, but they filled out a C cup. They were still perky. Likely they were still on the erogenous radar, though she couldn't guarantee that.

Other than her yearly gynecology exam, her breasts hadn't been touched by a pair of male hands in years. Nor had any other of her intimate zones. It was only natural she'd react to the sexy cowboy lawman who'd come riding to her rescue in a black pickup truck.

Only, if she were honest with herself, she'd admit it was more than just physical attraction. Wyatt was like no one she'd ever met before. Laid-back. Cool under stress. He had that take-charge cop manner about him without being boorish. Protective, but not authoritative. Sexy, but not arrogant.

Of course, she barely knew him, so that might all be a practiced facade.

Kelly stepped into the tub and slid beneath the water, letting the fragrant heat caress her. She closed her eyes and let the strain seep from her muscles and rational thoughts regain control of her mind.

She was a bit infatuated with the Atlanta detective who knew his way around a skillet, but she wouldn't have to deal with that for long. She'd likely never see him again after tomorrow. He had his problems. She had hers.

Her traitorous thoughts betrayed her as she slid the soapy cloth over her abdomen. What would it have been like if Wyatt had actually kissed her?

Passionate and fiery or slow, wet and romantic? Or maybe he'd be a downright lousy kisser like the quarterback she'd dated in high school who'd taken icky to new levels of disgusting.

Somehow she couldn't imagine Wyatt as icky, but perhaps she should kiss him goodbye when she left him tomorrow and find out. Solely in the name of research.

Chapter Seven

Wyatt jerked awake, lurching for the covers as they were being jerked off the bed. "What the hell?"

"Morning, bro. You're on ranch time now. Gotta make hay while the sun shines, or at least grab a pitchfork and toss some of it around."

"Watch it, half-pint. I can still wrestle you to the ground with one arm."

"Try it."

Wyatt jumped out of bed in his boxers and greeted Dakota with a quick manly hug and a couple of arm punches. The actions didn't begin to convey how glad he was to see his championship bull-rider younger brother.

"How did you find out this early that I was here? It's…" He reached for his watch and checked the time. "Nine o'clock! I figured it was about six. This old bed must be more comfortable than I remembered it being."

"It's eight our time."

"Right. I forgot to reset the watch when I changed time zones. Still early for a house call. What time did Troy phone you?"

"He didn't. I was headed over to Bob Adkins's

spread. He's having trouble with the gears in one of his tractors and I promised to take a look at it."

"Still handy with a wrench, I see."

"Comes from taking my bike apart when I was five and from watching Dad work on that old Chevy he had when we were kids. You remember that rattletrap?"

"I remember." Wyatt had learned to drive in that car years before he was old enough to have a driver's license. Not that he was ever allowed to venture outside the main gate of the ranch.

"Bob Adkins?" he asked Dakota. "That name sounds familiar."

"He owns a neighboring ranch. He and Dad have apparently been friends for years. Anyway I saw a new truck parked in Dad's drive and stopped to check it out."

"No secrets on the ranch."

"We look out for one another. I thought he was kidding when he said the pickup belonged to you. But he was too excited for it not to be true."

"I tend to excite people. It's a curse."

"You tend to be full of bull."

Wyatt raked his fingers through his short, unruly hair, knowing from experience he'd likely only rumpled it more. It was easy being with Dakota, a total contrast from his reunion with Troy. With Dakota, he felt like family. With Troy...

No use to go there again.

"What's it like sleeping in your old bedroom?"

"I didn't worry until I started craving baseball cards and stale Halloween candy," Troy said, keeping it light.

"Did you look? There might be an old Tootsie Pop hidden in here. Dad said I should let you sleep, that you'd gotten in late last night."

"You were never great about following instructions."

"That's what Viviana says. But, hey, I brought coffee." He reached behind him to the top of the bureau where he'd obviously set two pottery mugs of brew while he'd jerked the covers from the bed. He handed one to Wyatt.

Wyatt sipped and swallowed. "Hot, strong and black, just the way I like it."

Dakota straddled an old straight-back desk chair that Wyatt used to sit in to do his homework. "Why didn't you let us know you were coming for a visit?"

"I was afraid you guys would do something stupid, like rush into my room while I was peacefully sleeping and jerk the covers off of me."

"Where would you get a weird idea like that?" Dakota drank his coffee while Wyatt pulled on the jeans he'd thrown across the foot of the bed when he'd shed them last night. He'd crashed after the pancakes, too tired to shower.

And then he'd lain awake a solid hour fighting back good and bad memories and trying to figure out his unreasonable attraction to a woman he'd just met.

"Dad says you showed up last night with a good-looking damsel in distress and her kid in tow."

Right on cue. "Did Troy mention that there's a gigantic tree through the roof of the house they were moving into?"

"He did, and that her car had been stolen. She was lucky you were at the truck stop."

"I was thinking you, me and Dylan might be able to clear that tree off her roof."

"We could, but a job like that is a lot easier to do with the proper equipment," Dakota said.

"Meaning more than what we have here at the ranch?"

Dakota nodded. "I have an ex-bull-rider friend with a tree trimming and removal business just north of Mustang Run. I don't think he gets a lot of business in January. I can check and see when he can get to it. I'll let him know it's an emergency."

"I'd appreciate that." Kelly might see this as overstepping the bounds of their fragile relationship, but she needed the hole covered before more rain, sleet, squirrels, birds and who knew what else dropped into the house.

"We're flush with power tools and expertise, though," Dakota said. "Just in case you decide to help her with repairs. Dad and Dylan not only built Dylan and Collette's house but they built a starter cabin for Tyler and Julie, all before I got here. They had some help with the finishing, but did all the foundation and framing work themselves.

"And in the past six months, they've helped me build a cozy cabin for Viviana, Briana and me."

Wyatt knew the full story of how his bull-rider brother had found out he had a kid with the beautiful Dr. Viviana Mancini, months after the birth of his daughter, Briana. He'd saved both their lives and from the phone conversations he'd had with Dakota, he knew that the guy was absolutely mad for Viviana and loved his daughter with a passion that had even surprised him.

"We decided to start small and add on to our cabin later," Dakota continued. "Just a kitchen, living area, master bedroom and a nursery for Briana for now, but it sits on top of a hill with a view of Dowman Lake."

Dowman Lake, Troy's favorite fishing spot when

Wyatt was a boy. He'd kept a small motorboat there, only big enough for two. Wyatt had felt like he was ten feet tall when Troy had taken him along. They'd talked about man things like the Longhorns' chances for having a winning season and how to clean and skin a catfish.

A lifetime ago. Wyatt finished his coffee. "Sounds as if you've decided to live on the ranch permanently. You were undecided last I heard."

"We'll likely have at least a condo in Austin. My gorgeous physician bride is taking some time off, but eventually she wants to join the E.R. staff of a major hospital on a part-time basis. She loves her work and she's good at it."

Viviana. Briana. Julie. Wyatt might need a score-card to keep up with the family if it kept growing. And it obviously was, since Dylan's wife, Collette, was expecting.

"What about you, Dakota? Giving the bulls a hiatus?"

"Had to." Dakota grinned. "I'm still on my honeymoon."

"For six months?" Wyatt knew detectives whose marriages hadn't lasted that long. "That must be some honeymoon."

Dakota grinned. "Viviana is some woman."

"She must be to have tamed you."

"I'm sure you'll meet her and Briana before the day is over."

Dakota, who'd ridden the rodeo circuit with wild abandon, gathering silver buckles like they were coins, had nabbed the biggest honor of all a couple of years back when he'd won the Bull Riding World Championship.

Now he had a wife and a baby and the responsibility didn't seem to worry him at all. Evidently marriage and family were right for him. Wyatt couldn't see that in his own game plan.

"How long are you here for?" Dakota asked.

Now they were getting down to the nitty-gritty. "I'm not sure," Wyatt admitted.

"When do you have to be back on the job?"

"I don't." There was no reason to lie to Dakota. "I handed in my resignation before I left Atlanta."

"By choice?"

"Yeah."

"I thought you loved what you were doing."

"I did, but I have another interest to pursue."

"Like what?"

"Finding Mother's killer."

Dakota groaned. "You still think it's Dad, don't you?"

"The evidence says that. I'm keeping an open mind."

"He's innocent, Wyatt. I was right there where you are until about six months ago. But once you spend some time with him, you'll see how much he loved Mom and how determined he is to find her killer."

"Good. Now I'll be here to help him."

"Have you told him that?"

"Not directly, but he asked me to look over the information he's collected and I agreed to give him my opinion."

"I hope you do find the real killer, Wyatt. Mother deserves justice and Dad deserves some peace of mind. But don't heap more pain on an innocent man. He's the first to admit he made mistakes with us, but he didn't kill Mom."

"I'm a homicide detective, not a witch hunter."

Jaci's voice and the sound of little feet skipping down the hall wafted through the crack beneath Wyatt's bedroom door. With her daughter awake and going strong, Kelly was likely pacing the floor waiting on Wyatt to drive her and Jaci into town—unless she'd already talked Troy into doing that.

"The natives are probably getting restless," Wyatt said. "I'd best get moving."

"Me, too. Bob will be wondering what happened to me. But I'll check with my friend about removing the branch before I leave."

"Thanks. It would be great if he could get to it today so that Kelly can get some kind of tarp over the hole."

Dakota opened the door and stepped into the hall. Wyatt was already rummaging through his duffel for a clean shirt when Dakota stuck his head back into the room.

"Welcome home, Wyatt. And may I be the first to say it's about damn time?"

THE CHATTER COMING FROM THE KITCHEN was several decibels louder than a rock concert by the time Wyatt was showered, dressed and striding in that direction. Troy's husky voice seemed almost a growl compared to Jaci's high-pitched one. Kelly was laughing. And a lyrical voice with a slight Southern drawl was tangled in the mix.

He stepped inside the door and studied the unfamiliar, familial scene. Dakota was standing near the back door with a finger in one ear and his cell phone at the other. Troy was setting the table.

A shapely blonde with a dancing ponytail was pulling a pan of golden biscuits from the oven. Jaci was perched on a tall kitchen stool, swinging her legs and watching her mother whip a bowl of eggs.

Kelly was in jeans, presumably the ones she was wearing last night since she'd had no luggage. But he'd never seen the nubby, emerald-green sweater she'd paired with them. It looked great on her, but he couldn't imagine what hat she'd pulled that out of.

Wyatt paused in the doorway, suddenly struck with a sensation of déjà vu so intense he grew dizzy. A song he hadn't heard in years echoed inside his brain. A song his mother had sung countless times while she was preparing breakfast, often accompanying the tune with a dance step or two.

The voices, the laughter, the heat from the oven, the activity around the gas range brought it all back as if it were yesterday. He and his brothers gathered around the table, Dakota usually the last one there, complaining that he couldn't find his backpack.

His father would show up at the very last minute, having already put in a few hours' work on the ranch. He'd stamp the mud off his boots at the back door and come bounding in with news of a new foal or a cow that he'd had to pull out of a gully down by Willow Creek.

The ranch would need more rain or less rain. The day was going to be a scorcher or it would likely be sleeting by noon. No matter if the news was good or bad, Troy would stop and give his wife a kiss. And then he'd smile and fill his plate, bragging that their mother was the best and prettiest cook in the state of Texas.

"That was Cory calling me back," Dakota said. "Here's the roof scoop."

Dakota's announcement yanked Troy from the reverie and grabbed the attention of the others in the room.

"He can have one of his crews remove the branch

from the roof this afternoon. In addition, he can install the type of blue roof sheeting that FEMA uses to keep the house from further damage from the elements."

"Great," Kelly said. "Am I supposed to meet him there?"

"I can meet him there for you, unless you want to help supervise the work."

"I'd only get in the way."

"No problem. I'll let you know when the roof is cleared and covered."

She finally noticed Wyatt standing in the doorway and her smile lit up her face. He had that crazy stirring again, as if he'd touched a live wire and current was zinging along his nerve endings.

"One more for breakfast?" Kelly asked.

"Definitely," he answered. "No red-blooded American can resist homemade biscuits—unless he's offered pancakes."

Kelly blushed at the reminder of their midnight meal.

"Biscuits with homemade gravy," the perky blonde added, "but no guarantees on the edibility of that. I haven't totally mastered the art of smoothing out the lumps."

She dried her hands on a paper towel as she maneuvered around the table and walked over to greet him. "I'm Julie, Tyler's wife."

"Good to meet you, Julie. I'm Wyatt, Tyler's brother, who hasn't had homemade gravy in so long, I'll enjoy the lumps."

He held out his hand. She ignored it and pulled him into a warm embrace.

"Tyler talks about you all the time. He is going to be so envious that I'm getting to visit with you in person."

"The pleasure is all mine. Any word on when he'll be back in the States?"

"Nothing definite, but hopefully he'll be fully discharged and back on the ranch for our first anniversary in March. I'm counting the days. Kelly can fill you in. I've bored her with nothing but talk of Tyler for the last half hour."

"I haven't been bored for a second," Kelly countered. "You have all been great help this morning. I especially love this sweater you *gave* me, Julie."

"*Lent* you," Julie teasingly corrected.

Julie was exactly as Wyatt's brother Tyler had described her. Bubbly. Exuberant. And obviously as in love with Tyler as he was with her. They'd met on Tyler's leave last spring and had married before he returned to his tour of duty.

Kelly poured the eggs into a hot skillet. "I feel as if I've parachuted into a convention of Good Samaritans."

Wyatt felt as if he'd plunged into the pages of a bad science fiction novel and he was the alien—the only character who hadn't bought into Troy's innocence and swallowed the perfect-family pill.

Kelly on the other hand seemed to fit right in. She was busily scrambling eggs as if she'd cooked for the Ledger household every morning of her life.

"I talked to Sean a few minutes ago," Troy said. "He and Eve are driving over for the welcome home celebration tonight."

"So we'll all be here," Dakota said. "Guess I'd better tell Dylan to smoke a brisket."

"I've already got that covered," Troy said.

"I'll bring chocolate pies," Julie said. "And I'll make a giant potato salad."

A celebration with the whole family—though they

hadn't really been a family in years. The Ledger sons had been separated like cattle herded into alternating branding pens. Only, they hadn't even ended up in the same state.

Wyatt would love bonding with his brothers. It was the father-led family idea that tasted so bitter on his tongue. The fact that he was the only one who saw it that way made it doubly acidic.

"I've talked to the movers," Kelly said when he walked over to the counter and poured himself a cup of coffee. "They ran into some delays yesterday and won't get into Mustang Run until around noon."

"Then what will they do with the load?"

"Julie told me about a storage-unit facility in Mustang Run. I called and they have several climate-controlled units available. I have to meet the moving van there to pay the first month's rent and sign the paperwork, but I can store everything until the house is ready for me to move in.

"And on your father's suggestion, I've called my bank and had them block all transactions until I can get in to close my account and open a new one. I think that covers most everything you missed while you were sleeping in."

She gave the eggs one last stir and then spooned them onto a serving platter.

"You've been busy."

"Jaci woke me up at seven, so I've had plenty of time to get organized. Now I'm just waiting for the sheriff to call and tell me that he's recovered my car."

"You're in an upbeat mood this morning."

"Your family has inspired me. I'm thinking positive."

She said it with authority as if she wanted to make sure he didn't do or say anything to bring her down.

"You know, Kelly, there's a new apartment complex in town," Julie said as they all sat down at the table. "Their sign says that every unit has its own garage and a small patio in the back. I don't know about the cost or the lease requirement, but I can drive you in to look at the apartments after breakfast if you want."

"It's none of my business," Troy said, "but why waste the money? There's plenty of room right here on the ranch. Jaci can have her own bedroom and acres of room to play outside on sunny days. You can even take her horseback riding."

Jaci's eyes lit up. "Where are the horses?"

"They're still in the horse barn," Troy said, "but later today, they'll be in the horse pasture."

"What's a passer?"

"A pasture is a big fenced yard for horses and cows."

"Can I see the horses? Please, Momma. *Please.*"

"We'll see," Kelly said. "And thanks for the offer to stay on here, Troy, but that's taking ranch hospitality a bit too far."

"The offer will stay on the table, in case you change your mind. Unless that tree damaged the support beams, my sons and I can probably repair that damage in a few days and have the house ready for you to move into."

"I definitely can't ask you to do that."

"You help your neighbor, they help you. That's the cowboy way."

Wyatt stayed out of the conversation. He might consider one of those apartments for himself. He wasn't sure how much family he could take before he started to gag. Then again, if the food was always this good, he might be tempted to stick around.

He was on his third biscuit when his cell phone rang. He pulled it from his pocket and checked the caller ID. Sheriff McGuire. He excused himself from the table and took the call in the family room.

"Is Kelly Burger still at the ranch?"

"She is."

"Good. I tried phoning her cell number, but she didn't answer. Can you call her to the phone?"

"Is this good news or bad?"

"Let's just say it's worrisome."

And when a sheriff said that, the news was always bad.

Chapter Eight

"We have your car."

Kelly took a deep breath and exhaled slowly, relieved by the news, but too wary to celebrate yet. "Was the thief still driving it?"

"No, he'd abandoned it. The engine was cold so he'd been gone awhile before the vehicle was spotted."

"What condition is it in?"

"Busted trunk and driver-side door locks are the only visible damage. There are a couple of pieces of luggage, a box of toys, and a stack of hanging clothes still in the trunk, along with the spare tire and the usual tire changing tools. We didn't find a handbag."

No surprise there.

"Did you check inside the car?"

"The glove compartment was cleaned out, but there were a couple of sleeping bags in the backseat along with some books and toys. The cooler in the floor of the backseat still had a quart of milk in it."

"What about my daughter's booster seat?"

"Still there."

Good. One less thing she wouldn't have to purchase. "What about my computer?"

"No sign of that. I suggest you call your bank and have your account blocked—just to be on the safe side."

"I've taken care of that."

"If you don't have one of those identity-theft policies, you might want to look into that, too. Operate on the basis that the thief has access to everything in your computer, even if it's files or emails that you think have been deleted."

"Good point." It made her uncomfortable that the laptop was in the hands of a thief, but the computer was new. She hadn't used it for any banking or credit card purchases, so she should be safe there. "Where was the car found?"

"This is the part that concerns me, Kelly."

Her stomach knotted. "Why?"

"Brent spotted the vehicle just a few minutes past eight this morning. He was in the area, picking up donuts and coffee at the convenience store when he decided to swing by and check out the damage to your house. Your stolen car was parked in your driveway."

So the perverted thug had shown up at her house. A wave of dread and fear gushed through her veins. What if the tree hadn't fallen onto her roof? What if she and Jaci had been in that house when the lunatic had been there?

"Why would he return the car to my address?"

"I'm hoping you'll tell me that."

"How would I know..."

The answer hit her before she finished asking the question. McGuire thought she was lying or at least holding something back. He must have had her investigated the way Wyatt had. Or maybe Wyatt had lied about keeping her secrets and shared with the sheriff what she'd confessed to him last night.

A choking mix of fury and fear lumped in her throat. "I was just sitting out a thunderstorm in a café when my car was stolen," she said icily. "That's all I know to tell you."

"Okay, settle down, Mrs. Burger. As long as you're leveling with me, you have nothing to worry about. I'll get to the bottom of this."

"Where does this case weigh in on your priority scale?" she asked, voicing concerns Wyatt had raised.

"You needn't worry about that. I take risks to all the citizens of this county seriously, Mrs. Burger. Your car has already been towed to the forensic center. It will be thoroughly examined for fingerprints or any other evidence. That information along with descriptions provided by you, Wyatt, and Edie should go a long way in helping us identify the perp. If he's still in the area, he'll be arrested."

That couldn't happen too soon for her. It didn't resolve her issues with Wyatt. "When can I get my car back?"

"You can pick up your belongings as soon as the evidence check is completed. I'll have the investigating deputy call and give you a heads-up. But I need to keep the car a couple of extra days."

"Why?"

"A precaution—in case we need to take a second look at it. In the meantime, you be careful and if the thief tries to make any personal contact with you, call me immediately."

"Believe me, I will."

"Just so we're on the same page, Mrs. Burger, I don't want to find out after the fact that you know who this guy is or that you weren't a random victim. So if there's anything you haven't told me, now's the time to come clean."

"I'd never seen the man who stole my car until I walked in that truck stop last night. I have no reason to suspect that he knew me."

"In that case, expect a call from the deputy later today as to when you can pick up your possessions."

The phone slipped through Kelly's shaky hands as she broke the connection.

Wyatt caught the phone. "What did McGuire have to say?"

"Get your jacket, Wyatt, and I'll get mine. We need to talk—in the backyard, out of hearing distance of Jaci and your family."

A BRISK WIND MADE the day seem even colder than the thirty-three-degree temperature registered on the back-porch thermometer. Kelly seemed not to notice as she stamped down the steps and started across the yard in her lightweight wrap.

Fortunately, Wyatt had remembered her lack of luggage and retrieved an extra hunting parka from the back of his truck.

He hurried to catch up with her. "Put this on." He tried to hand her the jacket, but she kept her arms hugged tightly about her chest.

"I'm not cold."

"Then that's a weird shade of blue lipstick you're wearing." He draped the coat around her shoulders. "I take it the sheriff delivered bad news."

She stormed away again, this time stopping beneath a mulberry tree. Her stare could have frozen hot ashes. "Did you call the sheriff?"

"No. He called on my phone. He said he'd been

trying to reach you on yours, but you weren't answering."

"No, I mean did you call him last night after I'd gone to bed? Did you tell him about Emanuel Leaky?"

So that's what this was about. He took both her hands in his so that she wouldn't march off again. "I promised that I wouldn't say a word about that to anyone unless it was to save your hide. I don't lie, Kelly, and I don't break promises unless I have a damn good reason for doing so.

"I also don't read minds, especially women's, so how about leveling with me about what's going on?"

"Brent found my car."

"Brent, as in the sheriff's deputy that we met last night?"

"Right."

"Was it wrecked?"

"No. It's in almost the same condition as when he stole it. Almost everything that was in the car appears to still be there, though he did help himself to my handbag and computer."

Which should have been good news. "There must be more."

"Oh, there's more, all right," Kelly said. "The pervert left my car parked in my own driveway."

"That's bizarre."

"So bizarre that now the sheriff thinks I must know more than I've told him. Either that or he knows about my connections to Leaky and thinks this is somehow related."

A possibility that Wyatt hadn't totally ruled out. "I seriously doubt that McGuire took the time last night to have you investigated. He'd have had no reason to invest the time or the resources on a young, single mother whose car had been stolen. It's the thief's unusual behavior that's made him suspicious."

She pulled away from him and exhaled slowly, releasing a stream of vapor from her warm breath. "What possible reason could the man have for returning my car to my house unless he'd planned to harm me or Jaci?"

"He may have wanted to intimidate you, the same way he wanted to get under the skin of the waitress in the truck stop. The way he tried to intimidate you when he stopped near your table on his way out of the truck stop. Some sick jerks get their kicks that way."

Not that he was buying that. Had Kelly and Jaci been inside when the thug had shown up…

Wyatt sucked in a cold breath as sordid images from past cases stormed his mind. The rape and murder of a coed last summer. The mangled body of the nurse who'd opened her door to a man she believed was a meter reader.

"I guess I should be thankful the sheriff is trying to stay on top of the situation and identify the thief," she said once she'd finished sharing the gist of their conversation.

And if he didn't, Wyatt would. "I'll drive you to the storage unit when you're ready. By that time we may be able to retrieve your belongings from the car."

"That would be great. Maybe Julie will watch Jaci while we're gone. They seem to have hit it off and I don't want Jaci to overhear anything that will frighten her."

"Then that's settled."

"I still need to find a place to live until the house is livable."

"Forget about looking at apartments, Kelly. The situation has changed. You're staying here at the ranch."

He'd come on like a cop, ordered instead of asking. He waited for the backlash.

But it was apprehension, not anger that he saw in Kelly's eyes.

"Are you sure, Wyatt? I've brought you nothing but trouble."

"It makes sense."

"I'll think about it."

He'd accept that for now.

They were both silent as they walked back to the house. Questions rolled through Wyatt's mind like a stampede of wild horses.

When had the perp made the decision to go to Kelly's house? He couldn't have gone straight from the truck stop or the car would have been there when Wyatt and Kelly arrived and discovered the damage to the roof.

Where had he gone once he deserted the car? Did he live nearby or had he stolen another vehicle? If so, from where? And why hadn't that theft been reported? Or did the sheriff know more than he'd told Kelly?

A rabbit hopped out of their way as they approached the back steps. A horse neighed in the distance. And Jaci's excited voice rang out from the house.

Wyatt had been in Mustang Run less than twenty-four hours and already he was immersed in family, crime, and a woman who monopolized his thoughts while creating a fearsome hunger in him that had nothing to do with food.

Atlanta seemed a million miles away.

JULIE EAGERLY AGREED to watch Jaci that afternoon. She even seemed delighted that Kelly and Jaci might stay on at the ranch for a few more days. Once that was settled,

Kelly went to look for Jaci and Wyatt. She found them on the side porch with Troy, stacking a fresh supply of logs onto a metal rack.

Jaci was wearing a bright red parka that seemed to fit perfectly and looked practically new.

When Jaci spotted Kelly, she dropped the small log she was holding and ran over to wrap her arms around Kelly's waist.

"Mr. Ledger says I can go with him to feed the horses if it's okay with you. Can I, Momma? Can I, please?"

"Well, you do have a nice jacket to wear."

"I'll keep a close eye on her," Troy said. "My grandson tags along with me to the horse barn every time he gets a chance. I'm good with kids."

"I can tell."

"So can I go with him, Momma?"

"If you promise to do what Mr. Ledger tells you."

"Yeah! I can go feed the horses."

Jaci let go of Kelly's waist and began to jump her way across the porch as if she were on springs.

"I hope you don't mind my lending her the jacket," Troy said. "My grandson Joey left it here last weekend."

"I don't mind at all," Kelly assured him. "Joey must be just about Jaci's size."

"Pretty close. He's almost seven, but he's small for his age. You'll meet him tonight. The whole family will be here."

To dine on the fatted calf, Kelly thought, just as Sheriff McGuire had predicted. Only their reunion celebration would be marred by the problems Kelly had brought into their lives.

Troy dusted his hands together to rid them of dirt and loose bark. "You should go with us, Kelly. Collette has added two new quarter horses to the herd and they're real beauts."

"I'd love to see them." And to make sure Jaci didn't get hurt. The only horses Jaci had ever been around had traveled in circles on a carousel.

"All right then," Troy said. "Let's get going."

"Yes, c'mon, Momma. Let's git goin'."

Jaci held tight to Kelly's hand as they walked toward the barn, but her steady stream of questions were for Troy.

"Can the horses come out of the barn and play?"

"Do the horses stay with their mommas?"

"What do the horses eat?"

"Do the horses bite?"

Troy patiently answered every question. Not only was he as good with kids as he claimed, but he looked so at home on the ranch that it was difficult to believe he'd only been out of prison for a year and a half. It was even more difficult to imagine that this easygoing rancher had murdered the mother of his own sons in cold blood.

But evil didn't always come in ugly packages. Luther Bonner had been an impeccable dresser with excellent manners. Yet he'd willingly worked for one of the most brutal, corrupt individuals in the country. And just as willingly sold him down the river to avoid punishment.

When they neared the horse barn, Jaci let go of Kelly's hand and ran ahead. Kelly hurried to catch up. The wooden door was propped open, and the odors of hay and horseflesh greeted her even before she got her first look at the animals.

Troy stopped at the first stall and scratched the nose of a magnificent steed. "I didn't forget you, Gunner. I'm just running late today, but I brought company."

Jaci backed away from the stall until she was pressed against Kelly's legs. "Horses are big."

"Not all of them," Troy said. "Come meet Snow White. She's not even a year old yet."

"Snow White's not a horse."

"This Snow White is." Troy walked down a number of stalls before he stopped in front of a beautiful white filly. "Snow White is the newest addition to the herd."

The horse pawed at the floor, sending hay and dust flying. Troy calmed her with a soothing voice. "You miss Collette, don't you? I don't spoil you the way she does. She'll be down to see you later."

"Let's give her some food," Jaci said.

"Good idea."

Troy let Jaci help scoop and measure the grainy feed. She bored with that task quickly and jumped into a mound of fresh hay at the back of the narrow barn.

"Is this the entire herd?" Kelly asked as Troy distributed the feed among the horses.

"This is all of the horses presently at Willow Creek Ranch. There's fifteen in all, but we have three new quarter horses stabled at Sean's ranch in Bandera that we'll be moving here in the spring. We're adding another horse barn, one twice as big."

"What will you do with so many animals?"

"Breed and train them for buyers. And Collette and Sean are working on ideas for a summer camping and riding program for underprivileged kids from the city."

"Is Sean another son?"

Troy nodded. "He's Joey's father. He started out as a stepfather, but the adoption was finalized two weeks ago. Joey's mother, Eve, was a widow."

Kelly knew all too well how difficult that could be, especially when there was a child involved. It made romantic relationships difficult, as well. Kelly had dated a few times, but she'd always ended up resenting the men for taking up the few hours of work-free time she preferred to spend being a mother to Jaci.

But then she'd never met a man like Wyatt.

"It's bitter cold out here. You should pay wranglers to feed these animals on days like this."

Kelly turned at the sound of a deep, breathy female voice. The slim brunette standing in the doorway was as sexy as the voice, though she was probably at least fifty.

Her designer jeans fit to perfection. Her jacket was trimmed in mink. The matching hat and scarf in a shade of rich purple set off a flawless complexion and dark, expressive eyes.

"If it's too cold for you, you could have waited inside," Troy said.

The woman looked from Troy to Kelly and then back to Troy again. "I didn't realize you had guests." Her tone was accusing.

"I would have told you had you called before dropping by. This is Kelly Burger and her daughter, Jaci. They're moving to Mustang Run, but they'll be staying with me for a while."

"That sounds cozy. I'm Ruthanne Foley," she said. "Troy's neighbor and *close* friend." The woman stared at Kelly as if she were her opponent in a fight-to-the-finish fencing match.

It finally hit Kelly what was going on. The woman considered her a much younger rival for Troy's attention. That fire blazing in her eyes was pure jealousy.

No one had mentioned that Troy had a lady friend. Kelly wondered if that would further complicate Wyatt's relationship with his father. But she'd clear this misunderstanding up quickly before the woman's jealousy caused a scene.

"Actually, Wyatt brought me to the ranch," Kelly explained. "Troy was nice enough to invite Jaci and me out to see the horses."

"Wyatt's here?" Ruthanne gushed as she walked over and placed a possessive hand on Troy's arm, her attitude softening now that she knew Kelly wasn't a threat. "Why is it I'm the last to know these things? I can't wait to see him."

"Wasn't he at the house when you drove up?"

"If he was, I didn't see him. I only saw Julie and she told me you were at the horse barn. She didn't mention that you weren't alone."

Ruthanne Foley. The name was familiar, though Kelly couldn't place where she'd heard it.

Apparently deciding the newest guest to the barn wasn't worth her attention, Jaci continued turning flips in the hay.

"Kelly is Cordelia Callister's granddaughter," Troy said. "She's moving into the Callister place, or at least she will be once the roof is repaired."

Ruthanne stepped away from Troy and stared at Kelly, her gaze cold and totally unreadable this time. "You're Linda Ann's daughter?"

"I am. Did you know my mother?"

"I've met her." Her tone had grown icy again.

If the rest of the residents of Mustang Run were anything like Ruthanne, no wonder Kelly's mother had moved away and never wanted to come back.

"Ruthanne's ex is Senator Riley Foley," Troy said. "The man who may be our next governor if you can believe the polls."

Now Kelly knew where she'd heard about Ruthanne.

From her mother, years ago. "My mother was on the senator's campaign team the first time he ran for state representative."

Ruthanne studied her perfectly manicured nails. "That was years ago."

"Many," Kelly agreed. "I turned ten during the campaign. I remember because Mother was on the campaign trail with Senator Foley and had to miss my birthday. She made up for it later with a trip to the State Fair."

Ruthanne slapped at a horsefly with the fringed end of her scarf. "Where is your mother now?"

"In Plano, near Dallas. She retired as dean of a small women's college in the Northeast a few years back. But she's still teaching a few political science classes in a local community college."

"I avoid politics entirely," Ruthanne said. "I've never met a politician who could be trusted."

"Mother is not that jaded," Kelly said, "but as far as I know she hasn't helped run a political campaign since then, at least not as an official member of the staff."

"If I remember correctly, she didn't last the campaign with Riley. I can't recall why he had to let her go." Ruthanne turned back to Troy. "I expect a dinner invitation while Wyatt is here. Give me a call. I'll make that chocolate cheesecake you like so much."

"Don't count on it," Troy said dismissively. "I can't make plans for Wyatt. He's got four brothers who'll all want a share of his time."

Ruthanne said her goodbyes with barely a glance Kelly's way. She left just as Julie walked into the barn.

"What frizzed her curls?" Julie asked.

"I think I did," Kelly said. "I'm just not sure how."

"Maybe she doesn't like sharing her boyfriend with other women," Julie teased.

"She made that clear when she thought I was here with Troy, but her dislike of me seemed to go deeper than that."

"Pay no attention to Ruthanne," Troy said. "She's never happy unless she's the center of attention. All that family money she inherited makes her think she's a queen."

"No wonder her husband bailed on her," Julie said.

"He didn't bail until he had plenty of money of his own and figured she'd done about all she could do for him politically," Troy said.

"How long have they been divorced?" Kelly asked.

"Since about a year before I was released from prison. And rest assured, there's nothing going on between the two of us—except for those casseroles and desserts she keeps bringing around."

"Troy is the casserole king," Julie teased. "All the widows at the church bring him home-cooked treats. Some days he has enough food to open a restaurant."

"Not *all* the widows. Mrs. Haverty crosses to the other side of the street if she sees me coming."

Julie laughed. "And you drive her mad when you smile and tip your hat to her as if you're best friends."

"People believe what they want," Troy said, "and about half of the town wants to believe the worst about me."

Kelly was reminded again that the grandfatherly man whose house she was living in—the man whom Jaci had so easily befriended—had served seventeen years in prison for the murder of his wife. A jury had convicted him. Even Wyatt, an experienced homicide detective, wasn't convinced he was innocent.

Troy was strong. She'd seen him just lift a fifty-pound bag of feed and toss it to the ground as if it were a five-pound sack of potatoes. And she suspected the ragged scar down the right side of his face hadn't come from working on the ranch.

She couldn't see him as a murderer, but she hadn't seen Luther Bonner as a gun runner, either.

"Let me know when you're ready to go look at those apartments," Julie offered again.

"Momma, look. Snow White likes the food we gave her."

Excitement bubbled in Jaci's voice. The ranch agreed with her. And there was so much room for her to play outdoors.

"I'd like to hold off on that for another day or two," Kelly said. "If the offer's still on the table, Jaci and I will stay on at the ranch for a few more days."

"You're welcome to stay as long as you want," Troy said.

Jaci's cell phone buzzed. Someone had left a message. So far only her mother, the FBI and Sheriff McGuire had this number. She stepped deeper into the barn to avoid the sun's glare shining through the open door.

A second later she realized she'd been wrong.

Someone else had this number and the words he'd texted made her blood run cold.

Chapter Nine

Miraculously, Kelly managed to hide her emotions from her daughter until she'd walked back to the house with her and Julie. She was determined not to say or do anything that would upset or frighten Jaci.

Julie, however, picked up instantly on the change in Kelly's demeanor. But, other than asking her once if she was okay, Julie let the matter drop. Kelly appreciated that more than Julie could know.

Wyatt's family was truly remarkable, and in spite of the tension between Wyatt and his father, Kelly had never felt such an outpouring of support.

But it was Wyatt she wanted to talk to now. She found him in the courtyard garden, sitting on the cold wooden bench and staring into space.

She sat down beside him and pulled out her phone, punching keys to bring up the disgusting message. "You might want to read this," she said as she handed him the phone.

She looked over his shoulder and reread the message silently.

Nice car, bitch, but not nearly as hot as you are.

Can't wait to see you naked and begging for my...

She turned away before the nauseating clawing in her stomach got worse.

Wyatt mumbled a string of curses. "Sorry," he said. "Cop talk, but I'd like to know how this pervert got your cell phone number."

"Likely from my computer. I emailed my new phone number to Mother. I had forgotten all about that until I saw this note. I should call Sheriff McGuire and let him know that I heard from this lunatic."

Wyatt stood, took her hands and tugged her to her feet. "Call him on the way into town. You need to go to the storage facility. I just need to escape."

"You won't be escaping, Wyatt. I'm your biggest problem now and I'll be with you."

His fingers tangled in the loose curls at her left cheek, lingering for heated seconds before he tucked the hair behind her ear. Her pulse quickened and she looked away to keep him from sensing how his touch affected her.

"I know this situation is hard on you, Kelly, but I can and will keep you and Jaci safe. All you have to do is let me."

"I can hardly turn that down."

Unless it meant dragging him and his whole wonderful family into danger. Then she'd be on her own again, and this time without the FBI to back her up.

MOVING THE FURNITURE from the van to the storage unit went much faster than Kelly had anticipated. So she was really pleased when Wyatt suggested they explore her new hometown while they waited on the sheriff's call saying she could pick up her belongings.

She stared out the windows of Wyatt's truck, enchanted anew with the town she'd visited fewer than half a dozen times in her entire life. Hilly, lakeside resorts were sprouting up all around the town, yet Mustang Run had managed to hold on to its small-town charm, especially here on Main Street.

The narrow street was lined with quaint boutiques, coffee shops, bakeries and an ice cream parlor, all tucked inside small clapboard shops that had been standing for almost a century.

Crates filled with string-tied bouquets of colorful blooms lined the walk in front of a florist. Antique dolls rested in wooden cradles in one storefront. Beribboned square-dance dresses decorated the mannequins in another.

"I love the way they've revived this area without losing its historic character," Kelly said.

"But some things have changed," Wyatt said. "There used to be a movie theater on one of these corners. I remember seeing *Batman Returns* there at least five times."

"I take it you were a Batman fan."

"Best crime fighter of all time." Wyatt stopped at a crosswalk for a rotund man and his two leashed poodles. "When was the last time you were in Mustang Run?"

"I was here briefly when Mother and I met with the attorneys to settle Grams's estate. That was ten years ago. I had to fly back to New Orleans the same day for a jewelry show, so I barely had time to check out the house I'd just inherited."

"What about before that?"

"I came in for my grandmother's seventy-fifth birthday. I was twelve at the time. Her friends threw the gala on the front lawn of her house. It was quite an affair.

Even Mother flew down for a day, and she detests Mustang Run."

"You must have come back here for your grandmother's funeral."

"The funeral was in Boston. When Grams's Alzheimer's began to worsen, Mother moved her to a nursing home near her so that she could make sure Grams was cared for without her having to make regular trips to Texas."

"You obviously didn't see much of your grandmother when you were growing up."

"We visited, just not in Mustang Run. Grams flew to Boston to see us twice a year, once at Christmas and once in August when the Texas summers got too hot for her. And a couple of times when I was still in elementary school and Mother had to travel out of town for a seminar or a conference, she'd send me to visit Grams. I used to tell her even back then that I wanted to live in Mustang Run one day."

"No wonder she left you the house."

"That I failed to maintain."

"Do you have insurance?"

"Yes. I'm just not sure I have enough. I called my agent. He's supposed to call me back on Monday."

"What did your Mother have against Texas?"

"Not Texas, Mustang Run. All she ever said was that there was nothing to do here. Mind you, my mother thinks a day without intellectual stimulation is like a day without carob. Mother never has a day without carob."

"Sounds disgusting."

"Carob's not that bad once you get used to it."

"That's what they say about broccoli, but you can't prove that by me. I'm a meat and potato kind of guy, but a few ears of corn on the cob or a pot of purple hull peas are okay every once in a while."

"What else should I know about you?"

"That I become a real grouch when I get hungry. How about stopping for lunch?"

"I'm still full from breakfast," Kelly said. Actually every time she thought of the repulsive text message she grew nauseous and she wasn't ready to trust her stomach with food. "But I could use a cup of coffee."

Wyatt pulled into one of the angled parking spaces. She hopped out of the truck, considered getting her jacket from the backseat but then left it. The wind had died down and with the noonday sun bearing down on them, her borrowed sweater was warm enough.

Kelly scanned the signs and storefronts until she spotted Abby's Diner.

"We should eat at Abby's. She and my grandmother were fast friends. Even when Grams's Alzheimer's progressed to the point she couldn't remember her, Abby called to check on her once a week. And for her birthdays she always mailed Grams a homemade sweet-potato pie."

"Then Abby's it is."

Neither his expression nor his tone indicated he liked her suggestion. "We can go somewhere else if you like."

He shook his head. "One spot in Mustang Run is as good as another."

He strode toward the restaurant, the muscles in his arms flexed as if he were gearing up for a fight—or a rendezvous with his past. But he was right, there probably wasn't anywhere he could go in Mustang Run where he wouldn't risk that.

Mouthwatering odors reached them long before

they entered the diner. Once inside, the noise level and tempting smells reached a crescendo. It was half past one, but all the tables and booths were taken and the two seats available at the counter were not together.

A wisp of a hostess with long blond hair smiled flirtatiously at Wyatt and added an exaggerated sway to her hips as she walked over to where they were standing. Good-looking cowboys were apparently still in style at Abby's Diner.

"There's a ten-minute wait," she said. "The food is worth it."

"Do you guarantee that?"

"If not, dessert is on me."

"Can't very well turn that down," Wyatt said.

As the hostess walked away, Kelly leaned in close enough to whisper in his ear. "If you play your cards right, dessert could probably *be* her."

"I could say the same for those two cowboys at the counter who are eyeing you."

She checked them out. One gave a little salute. The other only nodded and grinned. "They're just being friendly," Kelly quipped.

"Uh-huh. Ye-haw."

For a cop, Wyatt had a terrific knack for defusing the tension in a situation or in a day. And for making a couple of sexy cowboys seem as exciting as watching fish swim across a screen saver.

Five minutes later, the hostess seated them at a back table that was tucked away in a corner niche by itself. As crowded as the restaurant was, it actually offered a degree of privacy.

Wyatt chose the seat that gave him a view of the

door. "I always like my back to the wall. It's a cop thing."

That left Kelly with a view of a booth where three men wearing mechanic's overalls were shoveling down pie topped by mountainous meringue.

A middle-aged waitress set glasses of water in front of them and handed them menus. "The special today is chicken-fried steak with creamed potatoes, gravy and pinto beans. Or you can have a side salad instead of the beans."

"Just coffee for me," Kelly said.

"And I'll take the special," Wyatt said without bothering to look at the menu.

"With biscuits or corn bread?"

"Corn bread. And iced tea."

"I'll have it right out."

"You must be hungry," Kelly said as the waitress walked away. "Did you see the size of those chicken-fried steak orders coming out of the kitchen? The steaks were spilling over the edge of the plate."

"Nice appetizer size." He stared at a spot over her left shoulder. "Don't get too comfortable. We are about to have company."

Before she could ask who, Sheriff McGuire stepped into view.

"I'm glad I ran into you two here," the sheriff said. "It will save me a phone call."

"Does that mean I can get my things from my car now?" Kelly asked.

"Anytime after four. That's the latest word from my evidence team." McGuire slid into the empty chair kitty-corner from her. "They've finished checking the interior," he said, lowering his voice, though there was little chance of it carrying to the next table over the din of clattering dishes and noisy chatter.

"Any success?" Wyatt asked.

"Nothing of consequence."

"He must have left fingerprints," Kelly said.

McGuire shook his head. "Unfortunately, it's not as easy to collect a usable print as it looks on the CSI shows. Wyatt can tell you that. They did lift a couple of viable prints from the Corvette, but it may take a while to determine if they belong to the thief or someone with a legitimate reason for being in the car before it was stolen."

Kelly felt the disappointment mounting again. "Have you been able to trace the text message sent to my phone?"

"We're working on that. These things take time and if the text was sent from one of those pay-as-you-go phones, it's impossible."

A different waitress approached their table. This one was chubby with short graying hair, sparkling blue eyes and a smile that showed a row of tea-stained teeth.

She punched a finger into the sheriff's forearm to get his attention before propping her hands on her ample hips. "What are you doing hiding in the back corner?"

"Making new friends and avoiding the ornery cook."

"Just for that, you'll pay for your pie today, lawman."

"You'll change your mind about that as soon as I tell you who this is I'm sitting with."

The woman looked over both Kelly and Wyatt and then slapped her hands against her cheeks in surprise.

"Lands to Goshen. It's Wyatt. Sure can't deny you're a Ledger. You could have been cloned from Troy. He must be higher than the price of gas with you back in town. When did you get in?"

"Last night."

"I'm Abby," she said. "You probably don't even remember me. What were you when you left here? Twelve? Thirteen?"

Finally, Wyatt smiled. "Thirteen and how could I forget you? You used to give me and my brothers free ice cream if we snuck in while Mother was shopping."

She chuckled. "And then I'd tell you not to tell Helene I'd spoiled your lunch."

"We always did."

"She didn't really mind. Your mother and I were the best of friends. I taught her to make pie crust. She taught me how to grow my own herbs and how to put together a flower bouquet that looked twice as good as the ones from the florist. But even we never thought we'd end up practically kin one day. I guess you heard that my neice Viviana married your brother Dakota."

"I heard."

"Helene would have been tickled to death with that. I swear, I miss her to this day. Of course, I don't miss her the way Troy misses her. I don't 'spect he'll ever get over losing her. They had problems, sure, same as the rest of us, but I've never seen two people who loved each other more."

McGuire tore open a package of crackers from the skinny basket in the middle of the table. "You do go on and on, woman. Quit talking a minute and see how good your guesser works with the woman sitting next to Wyatt."

Abby cocked her head to one side and studied Kelly. "I give up."

"That's Cordelia Callister's granddaughter."

"Well, bless my bones. You're Linda Ann's daughter." Abby dropped into the empty chair and laid a hand on Kelly's arm. "It is so good to see a Callister back in this town. I was beginning to think they would have to bring in a wrecking crew and tear your old home place down."

"I hope to get the house fixed up and move into it," Kelly said.

"Your grandmother would love knowing that. She missed Linda Ann like crazy, but I can't say I blame your mother for kissing this town goodbye after that wedding fiasco."

Now Kelly was totally confused. "You must have Mother mixed up with someone else. She didn't get married in Mustang Run."

"No, and didn't that just turn out for the best?"

"Didn't what turn out for the best?"

"Her being jilted by that jerk so close to the wedding date. Right after that she met your father and Cordelia told everybody what a catch he was and how he and Linda Ann were soul mates."

"To his day, my mother claims she and my father were soul mates."

"Such a tragedy," Abby said, "him dying in that terrible car crash before you were born. But at least she had you and she didn't let the grief bury her like some folks do. She went right on to get her doctorate degree and really made something of her life."

"Mother's definitely an achiever. But she can't make pie crust."

"No, she was always the brainy one," Abby said. "Did you know that she scored higher on her ACT than any student who's ever graduated from Mustang Run High?"

"No. She never mentioned that." Nor had she ever mentioned being jilted at the altar by a jerk. Not that it mattered now, but it might explain some of her distaste for the town.

Abby excused herself a few minutes later and the sheriff followed suit. They walked away together with Abby laughing at something he'd said.

"I think there's a little flirtation going on between the two of them," Kelly said.

"Could be."

"You seem distracted."

"I was just thinking that with so much small-town familiarity around Mustang Run, I don't see how anyone could ever get away with murder, unless that someone is a person no one would ever suspect."

"Not even the sheriff."

"Especially not the sheriff. I'm thinking about my mother's murder, but the same theory may hold true for your situation."

"I'm not following you."

"The sheriff is working this case as if you were a random victim, but what if it's more than that?"

"It had to be random, Wyatt," Kelly argued. "The thief could not possibly know I'd stop at that truck stop. I didn't even know it beforehand."

"The car theft was random, but what happened after that may not be. It may have become personal after the perp discovered your identity either from the paperwork in your car or from the emails and files on your computer."

"So you think this perp, as you call him, followed up with his intimidation because of who I am?"

"It's not that far-fetched considering everyone knows everyone around here."

"I'd never seen that man before in my life."

"But he may have known your grandmother. For that

matter, he may have known your mother. She grew up around here."

"Grams has been dead for ten years and Mother hasn't lived in Mustang Run since before I was born. Only a very sick guy would carry a grudge that long."

"Like the man who sent you the text?"

"Point made." The complexity of possibilities was growing exponentially. "But why leave the car at my house untouched? If he's getting payback through me, why not drive it into a creek or at least knock out all the windows?"

"I doubt the visit was just to return your car."

No. He'd come back to do exactly what he'd threatened in his text. Her nausea returned.

"I'm just tossing around ideas at this point, Kelly. But maybe when he saw the downed tree and realized you wouldn't be returning that night, he decided it was a good time and place to dump the stolen car."

"And then what? Hike to the highway in a cold rain to try and hitch a ride?"

"If he lives in the area, he could have called a friend to pick him up, or he might have walked home or to a friend's house."

"It would have been a long walk."

"Not necessarily. I called the sheriff while you were in the horse barn. I needed him to clarify a few things, and he said there's a road about a mile behind your house with several freestanding houses and a fairly large mobile-home park."

So this disgusting person might have lived close to her grandmother. He might have terrified her as she grew older and made her afraid to go to the sheriff.

No. She couldn't see Grams letting some goon push

her around. Not with all the friends she had in Mustang Run.

Nonetheless...

"I'm beginning to understand why my mother hated this town."

HE POURED HIMSELF ANOTHER shot of whiskey and took it to the sofa. He still couldn't believe his luck, especially when yesterday had started off so rotten.

It was a sure sign the economy stank when you couldn't even make a living dishonestly. He hadn't had more than a few ounces of cocaine in the trunk of his car, a delivery for some rich broad in River Oaks who liked to inhale her afternoon delight.

It would have been a fast, easy buck with a drug high on the side if that idiot teenager hadn't run a red light and rammed into the side of his car.

All the cops had to do was check his license and run it though the system. Then they'd have been over his vehicle like cheese on an enchilada. A few measly ounces was enough to send him straight back to prison.

He'd had no choice but to take off running, dodging the traffic on South Shepherd and then cutting through a neighborhood. It had been pure luck he'd happened on the woman unlocking her Corvette. She'd practically thrown her keys at him the second she saw his gun.

But stealing the car belonging to Kelly Callister Burger had been like winning the lottery. Not only did he plan to make her squirm before he had his way with her, but she might just bring him enough change to take care of all his needs for the time being.

Money he'd been cheated out of almost twenty years ago.

He wondered what assassin fees were these days.

He'd been behind bars so long he was out of the loop.
He figured fifty grand was reasonable.

He downed another gulp of whiskey, picked up his
new prepaid cell phone and made a call. The phone
rang.

"Hello."

"I hope you're alone, because I have an offer you
can't afford to refuse."

Chapter Ten

There were two pickup trucks and one large work truck fully equipped with tree-trimming equipment parked in Kelly's driveway when she and Wyatt pulled up after lunch. Left with an hour and a half of free time before Kelly could get her belongings from her car, going by the house seemed to make more sense than driving all the way back to the ranch and then into town again.

Kelly had called to check on Jaci twice, and both times Julie had assured her that she was having a marvelous time with Jaci. Jaci's excited voice had convinced Kelly that the same was true for her.

Kelly studied the swarm of activity as she and Wyatt climbed from the truck to the clattering roar of gas-powered engines. Four muscular men in hard hats, goggles, jeans and work boots were on her roof, handling oversize chain saws with the ease she exhibited maneuvering a broom.

The damage looked far more extensive in the daylight. The main trunk of the oak had apparently been split almost down the middle by the lightning bolt Sheriff McGuire had mentioned. Evidently last night's storm had finished ripping it apart. Half of the tree had landed squarely on top of her house.

Dakota waved and moved toward them. "The fun started without you."

"I can tell," Kelly said. "Seeing this in the daytime, I guess I'm lucky the house is still standing."

"It may not be as bad as it looks," Dakota said.

"Good," Wyatt said, "because from here, I'd say the best bet would be to tear it down and start over."

Just what Kelly didn't need to hear.

"Cory wants to talk to you about cutting down the rest of the tree," Dakota said to Kelly. "He thinks... Well, I'll let him tell you. He's the one with his feet planted on terra firma and supervising."

Wyatt put a hand to the small of her back as they approached the house. "You and Dakota go ahead and talk to Cory. I'd like to take a look inside."

"Is it safe?" she asked.

"That's what I'd like to find out."

"There's a tree limb blocking the front door," she said, stating the obvious.

"Which is why I'll go in through the back."

"I don't have my keys with me."

"Vampires walk through walls." He flashed a wicked smile and walked away.

Dakota made the introductions.

Cory took off his goggles and propped a booted foot on one of the stump-size tree cuttings. "We've got a mess here, but it will all be cleaned up before we leave. Like I told Dakota, I think you ought to let me go ahead and cut down what's left of the tree while I'm here."

"It is an eyesore now," she agreed.

"It's worse than that. It's dying. See how the bark is falling off the part of the tree that's still standing? You'll have to take it down eventually to avoid the risk of it falling on the house, too. May as well let us do it now."

"How much is all of this going to cost?"

"If I hadn't seen the way Wyatt was looking at you a minute ago, I'd say a date for dinner. As it is, I'll just take those steaks Dakota offered—butchered and freezer wrapped."

Dakota adjusted his sunglasses. "You drive a hard bargain, man."

"I'll pay for the work," Kelly said.

"Don't worry about it. When I need a favor, I'll holler at Dakota. It evens out in the long run. We go way back."

But she and Dakota didn't. No one in this family had even met her before yesterday. They owed her nothing.

"So, do I take the tree out?" Cory asked.

"I guess it's the only thing that makes sense. So, yes. Chop my once beautiful tree to the ground."

"You can grow another just like it in another hundred years," Cory said.

"You tree men are all heart."

"I don't get you Ledgers," Kelly said, after Cory had walked away and started shouting orders to his crew. "Why go to all this trouble for me when you've just met me?"

Dakota shrugged. "Wyatt obviously likes you and he's our brother. It's the cowboy code to help when you can, fight when you have to and never squat with your spurs on. Take your pick."

In that case she'd take the first one. She was definitely attracted to Wyatt, but it couldn't possibly be more than just physical at this point. They didn't know each other well enough for it to be more.

Yet, she was already trusting Wyatt with her life and

Jaci's. She'd moved into his house. Had shared pancakes at midnight with him. She'd even confessed to helping the prosecution with their case against Emanuel Leaky.

All that within hours after meeting Wyatt.

Heaven help her if she'd made a mistake.

"Kelly, come here a minute, will you?"

"You're being paged," Dakota said.

She looked back toward the house. Wyatt was standing in the side yard, his shirtsleeves rolled up above his elbows despite the cold. His Stetson was pushed to the back of his head. Rumpled locks of copper-streaked hair fell about his forehead.

He absolutely stole her breath away.

"I'll be right there," she called back. "Thanks, Dakota. I guess I owe you a favor now."

"You can babysit Briana any night."

"That's a deal."

She strode across the yard to where Wyatt was standing, doing her best to avoid the worst of the mud and the surge of attraction that had just spiked inside her like a rocket at blastoff.

"I hope you didn't call me over to tell me the house should be gutted."

"Actually, I think Dakota is right. It could be a lot worse. The soaked carpet has to go. So does the wet Sheetrock and a good deal of the molding, but the house itself seems to be sound. I can't guarantee that from just a cursory look, but I can tell you they don't build houses like this anymore."

"Finally, good news. Better pinch me to make sure I'm not dreaming."

"I can do better than that."

Taking her totally by surprise, Wyatt leaned in close. The air evaporated from her lungs. When his lips touched hers, she trembled like a schoolgirl, desire tripping through her like shooting stars.

Her head was spinning, her knees weak when he pulled away.

"Sorry," he said. "Probably not the best idea to kiss you with an audience around, but I've wanted to do that ever since I found you attacking the innocent motorbike."

"You like it rough, do you, cowboy?" she teased, trying to recover from the desire still rocking her body.

"I'll take it any way you dish it out. But I actually called you to take a look at some boxes I found in the back room."

She followed him through the back door which he'd obviously had no trouble unlocking since the top half was busted glass. He led her to what had been Grams's bedroom.

Three cardboard boxes sat in the middle of the floor. Kelly's name was printed on each one with a black marker. They were dry, but there was standing water on the floor next to the closet.

"I was checking out that leak in the closet when I found the boxes. If you want them, we should take them with us before they get wet."

She stared at the boxes, hesitant to open them for fear they were the work of the maniac who'd left the text message.

"Mother paid someone to clear out the house after Grams died. She was supposed to donate anything of value to a local charity. The rest was supposed to be trash."

"Maybe she left these because they have your name on them."

"I'm a little gun-shy after all the negative surprises in the last twenty-four hours," Kelly said.

"Caution is always wise. Should I open one for you?"

"Please do, but watch out for slithering snakes, hairy spiders or stinging scorpions."

"A few of those may be in there even if the contents are legit. This is Texas."

Wyatt slit through the masking tape and opened the first box. A bright red homemade Valentine with glitter and dried globs of paint rested on top. The words *I Love You* were printed in uneven letters.

A choking lump settled at the back of Kelly's throat.

"Your handiwork?" Wyatt asked.

"Yes. I remember making that. I think I was about six at the time."

"Then I guess these boxes are keepers."

She nodded. "Grams must have packed these away for me before the Alzheimer's became so debilitating."

"I'll load them in the truck."

A kiss from Wyatt that suggested it was only the beginning and mementos from Grams.

Even the ravages of nature loosed on her roof and a maniac with a vulgar vocabulary couldn't spoil those.

At least not until the next blow fell.

DINNER HAD DEFINITELY BEEN a celebration. Brisket and ribs from the smoker, yams, potato salad, green beans, corn, coleslaw and the best homemade yeast rolls Wyatt had ever eaten. And that was even before they got to the homemade desserts.

Wyatt had stuffed himself again, and was still forking bites of pecan pie along with his second cup of decaf brew. The women had taken their desserts and coffee to the family room, leaving the kitchen to the men.

"Is there any news on the car theft?" Troy asked.

Wyatt filled them in about the stolen car being left at Kelly's house and about the text.

"That's extremely bizarre," Dakota said. "This guy must be a real kook."

"Possibly a dangerous kook," Dylan said.

"I agree," Wyatt said. "So does the sheriff."

"Are you signing on as protector?" Dylan asked.

"Unofficially. For the time being. I don't want her going into town alone."

"If there's anything I can do to help, just ask," Dakota said. "I could use a good fight."

"What's the matter?" Dylan teased. "Honeymoon getting too tame for you?"

"Honeymoon is going just fine, bro."

"I'll help any way I can," Troy said. "Let me know later. Right now I need some brisk air and to walk off about a thousand of those calories I ate tonight."

Wyatt finally pushed his pie saucer away as Troy grabbed his hat and jacket and left through the back door. "If I keep eating like this, I'll have to go out and buy some bigger jeans."

"We have the cure for that," Dylan said. "There are plenty of logs that need splitting."

"I thought all you guys did was ride around on horseback and look good in your boots and jeans."

"I can see how you'd think that," Dakota said. "But the looking good part just comes naturally."

"So what did you guys do, have a cook-off and marry the winners?" Wyatt asked.

"No, we had to teach them how to find their way

around a kitchen," Dylan said. "We just married the hottest women we could find."

Dakota lifted his coffee cup. "I'll drink to that."

"And the smartest," Sean added.

"Absolutely," Dakota agreed. "It's not easy sleeping with a woman every night who's smarter than you are."

"Too bad Tyler's not here tonight," Dylan said, "instead of on duty in Afghanistan. Then we'd all be together, right back where we started. The sons of Troy Ledger in the kitchen of the big house at Willow Creek Ranch."

"The sons of Troy and *Helene* Ledger," Wyatt added. Not that he thought his brothers had forgotten their mother, but they sure seemed to have forgotten that Troy had been convicted of her murder.

They ignored the facts of the trial completely. Either they'd never bothered to read the full transcript or they'd dismissed as unimportant some key points.

Troy had let the prosecution build a case on circumstantial evidence without offering anything substantial in his defense. He hadn't even explained Helene's having packed her bags the day she was murdered. Instead he'd acted as if he had no clue as to why she was leaving him.

"I know what you think, Wyatt," Dylan said. "But Dad didn't kill Mom. They loved each other."

"So how do you guys explain away the evidence— like the packed bags that indicated Mom was leaving Troy?"

"She could have been just going to see her parents," Sean said. "That's not the same as leaving Dad."

"Mother would be the first to tell us to stick by Dad," Dylan said. "Just give him a chance. Talk to him."

"I plan to spend lots of time talking to him."

"I can't argue with what you're doing," Sean said. "I never expected to set foot on this ranch again and with you coming from a Homicide background, it must make it even harder to see past Dad's conviction. But I agree with Dylan. Dad loved Mother. I'm more convinced of that every day. Eve thought the same long before she met me and she had the advantage of being one of his prison psychiatrists."

Fifteen minutes later they were still talking about the trial and getting nowhere. Wyatt was thankful for the sound of footsteps on the back steps that signaled Troy's return.

Troy stamped the mud off his boots and then shrugged out of his jacket and hat, hanging them both on hooks near the back door.

"Wind's picking up something fierce," he said as he headed for the coffeepot.

The talk turned to more agreeable topics and Wyatt was amazed at the satisfying lives his brothers had created for themselves and their families.

Dylan and Troy worked as partners, rebuilding the ranch and adding property and cattle to the spread. Dylan's wife Collette was due to deliver in two weeks. They wanted a houseful of kids.

Sean had his own horse farm in Bandera but was still in big demand all over the country as a horse whisperer—not that he called himself that. Their son Joey was in the second grade and loved horses almost as much as Sean.

"Any plans for when you hang up the bull rope for good?" Wyatt asked Dakota.

"Yeah," Dakota said. "Don't laugh or faint from shock. I know I dropped out of college after two semesters, but that was because I had bulls to ride. Anyway,

I figure we have one doctor in the family, we may as well have two."

"Whoa," Dylan said. "That's the first I've heard about you and the possibility of med school."

"I haven't mentioned it to anyone except Viviana and Troy before now, but if I can make the grades, I'd like go back to school and eventually get into an equine veterinary program, hopefully at UT, since it's close by."

"I'm impressed," Wyatt said.

Sean gave Dakota a high five. "And think of the money I'll save with a family rate."

Troy finally pulled a chair up to the table and sat down with them. "What about you, Wyatt? You must get some hellacious murder cases in the city."

"I *did*." He likely wouldn't get a better opportunity than this to admit to everyone at once why he'd really returned to Mustang Run. Dakota knew so it wasn't going to remain a secret forever.

"I'm no longer with the Atlanta Police Department. I resigned."

That stunned Troy, Sean and Dylan into arched brows and silence.

"That's a big move," Sean finally said. "Do you have a better offer or are you leaving law enforcement altogether?"

"I'm moving back to Mustang Run."

"Now that's what I'm talking about," Dylan said. "Dad and I can sure use you here at the ranch. If you don't like the idea of ranching, I'm sure Collette's father can sign you on as a deputy."

"I'm here to find out who killed Mother."

This time the silence grew deafening.

Troy was the first to break it. "I wondered when you'd finally get around to that. I'll share my findings with you and work along beside you or I can stay the hell out of your way. Your call."

"I'd like to see what you've done, but I have my own methods," Wyatt said. "I work best alone."

Troy's expression grew stony, impossible to read. "I won't interfere, but if you don't find the killer, Wyatt, I will. I won't rest until I know that justice has been served for Helene."

Troy pushed back from the table, stood and left the room as if the situation were settled. Tension hovered over the brothers, no one saying a word.

Finally Dylan broke the impasse. "There's your answer. He didn't kill her."

"Maybe not, but someone did. I won't stop until I find out who."

KELLY TUCKED THE COVERS around her very tired daughter. She and Joey had played together like old friends. They'd started out with board games and ended up in the middle of the floor with Jaci's dinosaurs, Joey's action figures and the wooden pawns of an old chess set they'd found in Sean's boyhood room while playing hide-and-seek.

At that point, Viviana had gone home to put a sleepy Briana to bed.

Kelly, Eve, Collette and Julie perused an old photo album filled with haunting family photographs of Troy, Helene and their five young sons. A picture of Helene in the rocker next to the hearth holding Wyatt in her arms was especially poignant.

Troy had knelt beside Helene, Wyatt's tiny fingers curled around one of his much larger ones.

Thirteen years and four sons later, Helene had been brutally murdered next to that same hearth. The disturbing comparison made Kelly uneasy as she bent to kiss Jaci good-night.

Jaci hugged her doll to her chest. "I like the ranch, Momma."

"I know you do, sweetheart."

Kelly liked it, too.

She liked the whole Ledger clan with their emotion, enthusiasm and the kind of zest for life she'd never experienced in her own family.

Kelly even liked Troy. She liked him a lot, but the murderous secrets hidden inside the house would never let go of him or Wyatt until the truth came out. And if Wyatt did find out that Troy had killed Helene, it would destroy the Ledger family. She wondered if he'd be able to live with that.

Kelly was totally infatuated with Wyatt. His kiss had awakened a need so raw and powerful that she couldn't think of him now without aching to touch him and to feel his lips on hers again.

Collette was waiting outside the bedroom door when Kelly tiptoed out. "Was Jaci all right with sleeping in a separate room?"

"She didn't seem to mind at all. I think it was Joey's telling her that he had his own room when he spent the night here that did the trick. They hit it off well."

"I noticed. The others left while you were getting Jaci ready for bed. They said to tell you they loved meeting you and Jaci and that they would see you soon. Dylan and I need to be going, too, but I wanted to make sure it was okay with you if we stop by after church tomorrow and help you guys finish off the leftovers. If you've had all the Ledgers you can stand for a while, don't be afraid to tell me."

"That would be great. There's enough food left to

feed half of Mustang Run. Besides, Dylan is a good buffer between Wyatt and his father."

"That's exactly what Dylan said. He understands what Wyatt's going though. I met Dylan the day he and his father both returned to Willow Creek Ranch for the first time in eighteen years. The first year of that had been while Troy was in jail awaiting trial. The next seventeen was after the conviction.

"They hadn't communicated in all that time. The strain between them was almost palpable."

"They've come a long way."

"They have. They talk every day." Collette made a face as she laid a hand on her extended belly. "Dylan, Jr., has a wicked kick."

"But it won't be much longer until he'll be kicking at the air instead of you."

"Two weeks and counting," Collette said, rubbing her belly again. "I am so ready. I've had the nursery prepared for months. Dylan refinished the cradle his mother had used with all the boys. It's at least a hundred years old, intricately carved and beautiful."

"I'm not surprised. The antique furnishings in the guest room are beautiful."

"Abby says Helene didn't have much money to spend on furniture back in those days, but that she had a knack for finding real treasures at garage sales and restoring them to almost museum quality."

"Helene must have been a fascinating woman."

"To hear Troy tell it, she walked on water. He didn't kill her, you know."

"How can you be so sure?"

"I just know. If you stay in this house long enough, you'll know he's innocent, too."

"How will I know?"

Dylan stepped into the hall. "I've got the truck heating so you won't get cold on the drive home. It's ready when you are."

"I'm ready," Collette said.

"How will I know?" Kelly asked again as Collette turned to go.

Collette held her belly with both hands. "Helene will tell you."

WYATT KNEW THAT JACI was sleeping in a separate room and yet he hadn't bothered to stop by to tell Kelly goodnight. She'd nervously anticipated that he would. She worried about how to handle the growing attraction between them, knowing how quickly the passion might escalate with no more than his touch to ignite it.

They were still virtual strangers, even though the intensity of both their situations had bypassed the normal get-acquainted period and sped the relationship ahead at a dizzying pace. She was afraid they were rushing into this too fast.

Yet now that he hadn't stopped in even to say goodnight, she worried that the kiss that had rocked her to her soul had meant nothing to him.

Kelly pulled back the covers and was about to climb into bed when Collette's disturbing statement about the murder pushed into her mind.

Helene will tell you.

What could she possibly have meant by that? It wasn't as if the pictures they'd looked at tonight could talk, although they did tell a convincing story of the Ledgers' happy, normal family life up until the point Helene had been murdered.

Helene had seemed happy in every one of the photos,

including the candid shots. But even those could have been posed—or altered.

But for what purpose?

More likely Collette's comment had stemmed from the hormonal shifts during pregnancy that made the photos seem extra revealing tonight.

Kelly walked to the sliding-glass door, pushed the curtain back a few inches and peered into the courtyard. Bathed in shadows and the gossamer shimmer of moonlight, the garden took on an ethereal appearance.

She was about to step away when she spotted Troy. He was sitting to one end of the ornate bench, shoulders stooped, his face buried in his hands. He appeared to be a man in agony, a strange reaction when he'd claimed to be thrilled to have Wyatt home again.

Perhaps the tension between him and Wyatt had come to a head after the others left. Or could it be that he was afraid of the truth his homicide-detective son was determined to discover? Even if he was innocent of the murder, could there be old secrets he didn't want uncovered?

The wind picked up, creating a ghostly wail. Troy didn't stir. Gooseflesh popped up on Kelly's arms as she closed the curtain and checked the lock on the glass door.

She crawled into bed and pulled the covers tight around her. In spite of all of her own problems, it was Helene Ledger who walked through her mind as she finally fell asleep.

KELLY WOKE UP in a pitch-black room, shaking from an icy blast that blew across her with hurricane-like force. The thick privacy drapes at the window fluttered like sails. The door to the outside must have somehow blown open. Only she remembered locking it.

Something creaked like old bones...or aging floorboards.

Kelly was not alone.

Chapter Eleven

Heart pounding, Kelly tried to escape, but the covers entangled her, pinning her to the bed. Then just as suddenly as the frigid wind had begun, it died. The curtain no longer swirled into the room. The creaking transformed into an angelic voice crooning a lullaby.

Diaphanous images appeared and moved across the ceiling. Slowly and methodically, one image emerged from the conglomeration. Helene, rocking her baby and holding him to her breast while she crooned a lullaby. The tune was mesmerizing and soothing.

The words were terrifying.

Family sins can kill. Stay alive. Stay alive.
Mothers always know. Stay alive. Stay alive.
Hold on tight to love. Stay alive. Kelly, stay alive.

The words and image evaporated in a burst of flame. Kelly kicked off the covers and sat up in bed.

She reached to the bedside table and flicked on the lamp. The room was just as it had been when she went to bed.

Her pulse was still racing. Her emotions were overwrought. Her nerves were rattled to the point of collapse, so frazzled that her mind had twisted the pictures from the photograph album into a slide show of mental horror.

But it was only a nightmare.

Still, she climbed from bed and pulled on her robe. She wouldn't get back to sleep until she assured herself Jaci was resting well and that her room was not too cold.

The house was peacefully quiet as Kelly took the few steps to Jaci's room, turned the doorknob and opened the door. Jaci was fast asleep, her breathing a gentle, reassuring rhythm that calmed Kelly like nothing else could have.

"Sleep well, sweetheart. I love you and I'll always be here for you."

But as she crept back to bed, she couldn't help but wonder if Helene had whispered those same words the last time she'd told her boys good-night.

WYATT STARED IN AWE at the charts, notes and timelines that took up one whole wall of the master bedroom. Whatever he'd expected from Troy's research, it hadn't been this. Wyatt had served on serial killer task forces whose investigations hadn't been this thorough.

"How long have you been working on this?" Wyatt asked.

"I started collecting facts in prison as soon as they granted me access to a computer. I wasn't this organized then, of course. My supplies were limited to a small notebook and a pencil that I had to be careful with. Sometimes it would take days to get it sharpened once I'd broken or worn away the point."

"You could have been a homicide detective if..."

The *if* hung in the air.

"One detective in the family is enough," Troy said.

"And in spite of all the research, I'm nowhere. Dead ends just keep piling on top of more dead ends."

"Dead ends can be deceptive," Wyatt said. "It's like a video game. When you hit a brick wall, you search for that one tiny opening that leads to the next clue."

"I've never played a video game in my life. I've watched Joey at it. It only makes me dizzy."

"Fair enough. Think of it as locating a calf that's lost in heavy underbrush. There's always a starting spot and then you keep following the leads until you find it. Equate the sound of the calf's bleating with motive. Both are always a good place to start."

Wyatt's mind raced ahead. Motive was what had led to Troy's being a prime suspect. That and the fact that the husband is always the first suspect when a married woman is murdered.

"Motive is a problem," Troy admitted. He picked up a yardstick and used it to point at a posterboard chart thumbtacked to the far left corner of the wall. "I've listed everyone Helene had contact with on a regular basis. Not one of them had a problem with her. Everybody liked Helene. That's why I think her murder had to be a random attack—a crime of opportunity committed by a complete stranger."

"That's seldom the case in a murder—"

Wyatt swallowed hard, biting back the word *Dad* before it slipped from his mouth. He didn't have trouble referring to Troy as his father. That was the reality of their relationship.

But he couldn't bring himself to call Troy *Dad*. Dad had been the person he counted on. The man he'd idolized. The man he'd been sure would always be there for him. That man no longer existed. His brothers had surely felt that same way about Troy when they'd first returned to the ranch.

"Random murders may be rare," Troy said, "but they happen on a daily basis in this country and they happened back then, too. Maybe the guy stopped by looking for a wrangler job and then decided to break in and steal something when he realized there was no man around. Your mother may have caught him in the house and he shot her."

"Nothing was missing from the house," Wyatt reminded him.

"My revolver was taken."

"Yes, and Mother's handbag had been in plain sight not six feet from the top of the bureau where you kept that revolver."

Evidence submitted in the trial emphasized that the weapon wouldn't have been loaded since Helene Ledger was terrified of having loaded weapons around her young sons.

The bullets for the gun were kept in a cigar box in the top bureau drawer. Whoever killed Helene either knew that ahead of time or found the shells while rummaging through the bureau drawers.

The weapon in question had later been found stuck between some rocks at the bottom of Willow Creek.

Wyatt skimmed the names on the random-killing suspect list. Most had been X'ed out for various reasons.

Three words stopped him cold—

Suspected paid assassin.

Jerome Hurley. Home address was in Mustang Run.

Wyatt tapped the word *assassin* with his fingertips. "Tell me about Jerome Hurley."

"Helene wouldn't have been killed by a paid assassin. She was a rancher's wife. She took care of you boys and took part in church activities."

Wyatt agreed. His mother was an unlikely target of a paid assassin. But that would be exactly the type of man Emanuel Leaky might hire to take out Kelly.

Troy used his yardstick to follow the progression to the next column. Hurley was convicted of raping a woman who was home alone on a ranch about forty miles west of the Ledger spread five years after Helene's murder. The X by his name was followed by the word *alibi*.

"What was Jerome's alibi?" Wyatt asked.

"Three people claimed he was having lunch with them at a burger joint in Austin at the time of the murder."

"Friends of his?"

"The two females were friends. The guy was his cousin."

"Was there any proof that the friends and cousin weren't lying?"

"The cousin's car was caught on a security camera leaving the restaurant parking lot. There were four people in the car. Two males, two females. The only one who showed up well enough for a positive identification was the cousin."

"Did Jerome have a rap sheet before that?"

"He'd been arrested on burglary and drug-related charges. Most of them didn't stick. He'd served less than two years combined on all his arrests."

"Where does the suspected 'paid assassin' label come in?"

"That accusation didn't surface until after Hurley was sent to prison for the rape. It was big news for about a week and then I never saw anything else about it in the local news or on the internet. I just noted it to keep my charts up-to-date."

"Was he questioned in Mother's murder?"

"Several times, but he was never arrested. McGuire had already zeroed in on me by then."

Troy might adore his daughter-in-law Collette, but it was clear from his tone that there were still some hard feelings on his part toward the sheriff.

Troy used the yardstick as a pointer again. "If you follow these arrows, you'll see specifics on Jerome's arrest records and his employment records."

Wyatt scanned the records, once more impressed by the methodical tracking of suspects. At one time or another Jerome had worked as a wrangler at least part-time for almost every major rancher in the area, including the woman he was eventually convicted of raping.

"He was working for Senator Foley at the time Helene was killed," Troy said. "Of course, Foley wasn't a senator back then. He was right in the middle of his first campaign for state representative."

"I vaguely remember that," Wyatt said. "Was Mother involved in that campaign?"

"No." Troy tossed the yardstick to the middle of a cluttered desk and stepped away as if he was finished with the discussion. He walked to the sliding-glass doors that opened to the same courtyard garden as the guest room did.

"Ruthanne and Riley both tried to get Helene involved in his campaign, especially Ruthanne. She finally persuaded your mother to drive to Austin and visit Riley's headquarters."

"Why did she decide not to volunteer?"

"I think someone must have rubbed her the wrong

way that day. When she got home she was adamant that she wanted no part of politics."

"I can understand that."

"I've wished a million times she hadn't felt that way. Then she might have been at his campaign headquarters instead of here alone when the killer showed up."

Wyatt turned away. He didn't want to be influenced by the emotion tearing at Troy's voice. He had to depend on cold, hard facts.

"Kelly's mother was on Riley's staff," Troy said.

Wyatt turned his attention from the chart to Troy. "Are you referring to Kelly Burger?"

Troy nodded and then worried the jagged scar on the right side of his face.

"When did you find that out?" Wyatt asked.

"Ruthanne showed up at the horse barn when I was out there with Jaci and Kelly yesterday morning. I introduced them and they talked about it. I got the impression there was not much love lost between Ruthanne and Kelly's mother. But that's no surprise. Ruthanne was never fond of any woman Riley spent time with."

There was a lot about Kelly that Wyatt didn't know. He probably should leave it this way since what he did know about her scared him to death. She sent his senses spiraling out of control every time she came near him.

Like that kiss yesterday. He hadn't planned it. It wasn't the time or the place for it. But his impulse control vanished and the first thing he knew his lips were on hers and she was turning him inside out.

Any cop worth his salt knew you should never get emotionally involved with a woman you were trying to protect. Emotions would make him lose his edge.

But now that kiss would be the proverbial elephant

in the room. No matter what else was going on, they'd both be aware that one touch could start the sparks flying again.

Create enough sparks and they would invariably flare up into a wildfire.

"You got awful quiet there when I mentioned Kelly," Troy said. "You're not having second thoughts about getting involved with her, are you?"

"I'm not getting *involved* with her. She needs protection and a place to stay. It seems reasonable to offer that to a homeless woman in jeopardy."

"I get the feeling she's been on her own with Jaci for quite a while. What about you? Do you have someone waiting on you back in Atlanta?"

"What if I do?"

"Then I think you may be in real trouble."

"Why is that?"

"Because I've watched four of your brothers fall in love. I know the subtle signs and you're exhibiting all of them."

"The subtle signs. That sounds like the title of a chick flick."

"You can pretend all you want, but there was an unmistakable current passing between the two of you when you got back to the ranch yesterday."

"I've only known her two days."

"Whether you've known a person years, days or hours has nothing to do with it. The spark hits in an instant. It was that way with me when I met your mother. It was that way for your brothers, too. Trying to deny what you're feeling only makes it worse."

Wyatt was definitely not discussing his love life or lack thereof with Troy.

The awkward conversation was thankfully inter-rupted by the doorbell.

"That must be Dylan and Collette," Wyatt said. "I'll let them in."

The doorbell rang again before he made it to the door. When he opened it McGuire was standing there. Unsmiling. A deadly serious expression on his face.

"Is Kelly here?"

"She is. Come in and I'll get her for you."

"You'd best sit in on the conversation, too."

"Is it that bad?"

Kelly stepped up behind him. "Is what that bad?"

McGuire tugged his hat low and narrowed his eyes. "Let's talk inside."

KELLY SAT ON THE SOFA. Sheriff McGuire had settled in the chair next to the window. Wyatt paced. Troy had volunteered to take Jaci outside to wait on Dylan and Collette.

McGuire crossed a leg over his knee. "I hate to have to bother you with this kind of news, especially on a Sunday, Kelly."

"I like to keep informed of exactly what's going on," she assured him.

"I asked the deputy working your area to keep an eye on your house, just in case the thief is stalking you. I figured that with the roof covered, he might think you'd moved back in."

Kelly got that sinking feeling again, as if she were hurtling down a rugged cliff with nothing to grab hold of.

"When the deputy pulled up in your driveway, he saw a guy take off on foot and disappear into that thick wooded area in back of your property. The deputy gave chase, and then he heard an engine grind before sputtering to life.

"By the time he reached the clearing, dirt was flying. He couldn't see the vehicle in the dark, but he caught sight of its back lights as it turned off onto that old dirt road that goes to the back of the Baptist church."

Wyatt stopped pacing and propped a booted foot on the hearth. "Did the house look as if someone had broken in?"

"The front door was wide open."

Wyatt's lips tightened to thin, hard lines. "If you don't stop this man, I will."

"We don't have any proof that the man seen running from Kelly's house was the man who stole her car or sent the text."

"She's being targeted," Wyatt said. "You know that as well as I do."

"What I know, Wyatt, is that you have no law-enforcement authority or legitimate credentials in this state, much less this county."

"Then deputize me," Wyatt said.

"I'd consider it if you weren't so personally involved in the case. As it is, you'd be more a vigilante than a cop."

"Bullshit."

This type of conflict was the last thing Kelly wanted. "I'm sure the sheriff can handle this, Wyatt."

"Exactly," McGuire agreed. "And if you'd let me finish, I have some good news, as well. It looks as if we have some reliable fingerprints."

"That's great news," Kelly said, trying to inject some optimism into the heated discussion.

"By the time the house is ready to move into, Kelly, we'll likely have made an arrest." McGuire uncrossed his legs and leaned forward. "In the meantime, I wouldn't advise staying at that house alone, not even in the daytime."

"Was the house ever broken into when my grandmother lived there?"

"Not once," the sheriff said. "Mustang Run is normally one of the most peaceful towns in Texas."

"Did Cordelia have problems or ongoing issues with anyone in the area?" Wyatt asked. "Maybe someone who tended to carry a grudge?"

"I see where this is going, but don't go putting store in the local gossip mill. Those women like to run their tongues. The men are just as bad. But all that talk of Ruthanne Foley wanting to run Cordelia out of town a few years back was mostly exaggeration."

"Why would she want to run my grandmother out of town?"

"Ruthanne pushed for the city to tear down some old houses near the park and sell the land. Cordelia opposed the plan and accused Ruthanne of just wanting to build a spa resort on the property. Cordelia won. The historic old houses are still standing. They're making one into a museum."

"Good for Grams."

Collette and Dylan drove up just as the sheriff was leaving. He looked delighted to see his daughter. She looked rested today and positively glowing. Even at eight months pregnant, Collette was stunning with her expressive eyes, high cheekbones and wild mass of fiery red curls.

One day Kelly would like to hear all about Collette's experiences while renting the Callister house, but not while Collette was pregnant—or while the man who was creating havoc in her life was still on the loose.

But the sheriff said they had usable fingerprints. Surely they would make an arrest soon.

Unless it was today, it wouldn't be soon enough to keep Kelly from moving out of the Ledger house. She'd look for an apartment tomorrow, and this time she wouldn't mention it to Wyatt until the rent was paid and she was ready to roll.

That was, if he ever stopped avoiding her long enough for them to talk. It was the first time she'd ever lost a man with a kiss.

BY FOUR ON SUNDAY afternoon, the temperature had climbed into the high sixties. In true Hill Country fashion, the wind that had hounded them for days had died to an occasional breeze that whispered through the needles of a juniper tree just outside the courtyard.

It was the perfect day for a tea party, and the courtyard garden was the perfect setting. Jaci had hosted the party for Troy, Kelly and two of her best-loved dolls. She'd used her favorite tea set, the one Jaci had insisted ride in the car with them when they'd set out for Mustang Run.

Jaci had served tiny cups of milk and the chocolate chip cookies she and Julie had baked yesterday. Kelly had sliced the cookies into fourths so that they'd fit on the tiny plates.

Once the cookies were gone, Jaci skipped away to retrieve a miniature plastic horse she spied peeking from behind a dwarf azalea.

She picked it up and brought it over for Troy to examine. "He has a broken nose."

Troy examined the toy. "I believe he does. That may be why Joey left him in the garden."

"Do your big horses break their noses?"

"So far they haven't."

"I hope Snow White doesn't break her nose."

"I do, too."

"Joey's not afraid of horses," Jaci said.

"Not now, but when he first came to the ranch, he had to get used to them, just like you will."

Satisfied with that answer, Jaci went back to exploring the garden.

"It's so peaceful out here," Kelly said. "It's as if you step into the garden and leave the world on the outside."

Troy stared at the sparkling fountain. "This was Helene's favorite spot. She planned every detail. Needless to say, it fell into disrepair when I was in prison. Collette spent hours out here working it back in shape."

"I'm sure Helene would be pleased with the result."

"I think so. I always feel closest to her when I'm in her garden. Some nights I sit out here in the dark and it's almost as if she's here beside me, trying to tell me something. I like to think she's just been waiting for her last son to come home."

A ghostly shiver raised the hairs on the back of Kelly's neck as Collette's prediction rolled through her mind.

Helene will tell you.

Perhaps like Troy, Collette felt Helene's presence when she tended the plants.

The haunting words from the nightmare began playing in Kelly's mind.

Family sins can kill. Stay alive. Stay alive.

Troy's cell phone rang, startling Kelly back to reality. She gathered the plates and cups while he talked.

"That was Dakota," Troy said. "He, Dylan and Wyatt are on their way back here for a family confab. Guess I'd better go start a pot of coffee."

Kelly hadn't been invited, but she was pretty sure the discussion would center on her and her tormentor. She doubted it had been Wyatt's idea to include his father, but she was glad they had.

Troy walked over to Jaci. "Thank you, ma'am. That was the best tea party I've ever been to. You make delicious tea."

Jaci grinned from ear to ear. "It was really milk."

"You fooled me." Troy tipped his worn black Western hat and left to join the men in the family. Thirty minutes later the sun dipped behind a cloud and Kelly and Jaci went back to the guest room.

Jaci took out her stubby crayons and drawing paper. "I'm going to color a picture of big horses," she said as she kicked out of her shoes and crawled into the middle of Kelly's bed.

Kelly retrieved the last of the boxes she'd brought home from Grams's house. The first two had held mementos, report cards, baptismal records and numerous small plaques and certificates that Kelly's mother had been awarded during her school years, mostly for academic achievement.

Setting the box on the edge of the bed, Kelly took the silver letter opener she'd discovered in the top dresser drawer and slit through the tape. She settled back against some pillows and spent the next hour skimming through dozens of photographs of Kelly's mother when she was growing up.

Linda Ann had been cute as a kid. By the time she'd become a teenager, she was gorgeous. Kelly found an envelope labeled Linda Ann—College Years.

She opened the envelope and dumped the contents onto the bed. There were dozens of photos of Kelly's mother in all kinds of settings and with various groups of friends. There were no couple photographs, which made it seem highly likely to Kelly that Abby had confused Linda Ann with someone else when she'd talked of her being jilted before she'd met Kelly's father.

Kelly was putting all the photos back in the box when she noticed a brown envelope stuck in the bottom folds of the cardboard. It felt empty, but when she opened it, she found an old newspaper clipping.

She had to turn it over before she discovered another picture of her mother. The page was slightly yellowed, but still Kelly's mother looked ravishing in a formal gown that dipped low from her shoulders.

Kelly read the caption beneath the picture.

"The mother of Linda Ann Callister announces the engagement of…"

The rest of the sentence was continued on the next line, but the next line had been cut off.

So Abby had been right. Her mother had come close to marrying someone else before she met her true soul mate.

The picture had been cut from the top right page of the newspaper. The page's edges were still intact.

Kelly checked the date.

Her stomach quivered.

There had to be some mistake.

Chapter Twelve

The date of the engagement announcement was seven months before Kelly had been born. But her father hadn't jilted her mother. And there would have been no wedding announcement. They were planning to elope to Las Vegas. He'd been killed in a car wreck before they could. Both her mother and Grams had told her that.

If this wedding announcement was authentic, then Kelly's mother would have had to become engaged to one man while she was pregnant with another man's baby. That was a far cry from the tale of undying love and soul mates that Kelly had always heard.

Her mother's affairs from long ago were none of Kelly's business—unless the man who'd jilted Linda Ann was actually Kelly's biological father.

This was too bizarre to even think about now, but when her life settled down to normal, Kelly planned to have a heart-to-heart with her mother.

Kelly closed the box and put it away just as someone tapped lightly on her door.

Anticipation made her heart skip a beat, but when she opened the door, it was Viviana, not Wyatt.

"You're wanted in the den," Viviana said. "The Ledger men have an offer you can't refuse."

WYATT PACED FOR A MINUTE before settling in one of the rockers near the fireplace. "This is the deal, Kelly. My brothers and I would like to repair your house and make it livable for you and Jaci. We won't all be able to work on it every day, but I think we can have it ready for you to move in after three or four weeks, unless we run into major support problems."

Kelly stared at Wyatt, stunned speechless by the announcement—and speechless didn't often describe her.

"Why?" It was the only word she could manage.

"You need the help, and we have the tools and the skills to see that you get it," Dylan said.

"It's really not that big a deal," Troy said. "January's a slow time on the ranch, not that there's not always work that needs doing on a spread this size."

Kelly locked gazes with Wyatt. "Is this okay with you?"

"Yeah, sure."

"It was his idea," Dakota said. "We just jumped on the bandwagon."

She understood Wyatt less by the minute. He'd barely spoken to her since yesterday's kiss and now he was rallying the troops to spend weeks working on her house.

Yet, as Viviana had predicted, the offer was too good to refuse. And by the time the house was done, hopefully, her mystery tormentor would be behind bars.

"I appreciate the offer," Kelly said. "And I accept, but only on the condition you let me pay you for your labor."

"Nonsense," Troy said. "We'd do the same for any neighbor who got a tree blown down on his roof."

This was moving too fast for her to absorb it all. "When would you start?"

"Nothing like tomorrow," Dylan said. "We need to get the roof and any other outside repairs done while the weather holds."

"The whole roof may need to be replaced while we're at it," Wyatt said. "There are leaks in the back of the house where the tree didn't touch the roof."

"I may have to wait on some things," Kelly said. "How much money are we talking about for building materials?"

"No problem," Dakota said. "Wyatt's taking care of—"

"We'll talk about money later," Wyatt said, cutting off Dakota. "No use to talk expenses until we know the full extent of the damage."

There was no mistaking where Dakota was going before Wyatt interrupted. Wyatt had obviously told them he'd pick up the tab. She had no intention of letting him. And no idea why he'd volunteer. They had to talk and soon.

"How about some food?" Julie said. "We still have plenty of brisket for sandwiches."

The men gave her suggestion hearty approval.

"I'll make hot chocolate," Viviana said. "And someone can build a fire. It's starting to get a bit nippy in here."

"A fire's a great idea. I'll get going on that," Troy said.

Jaci jumped up to follow Troy to get some logs from the side porch. "Let's git goin'," she said, mimicking Troy's Texas drawl.

She'd missed a lot by not having a grandfather in her life.

As the others left for the kitchen, Kelly walked over to where Wyatt was leaning against the hearth, intentionally moving into his space. Only inches separated them when he turned and met her gaze.

She saw desire flicker in the depths of his eyes. Heat suffused her body. Whatever was going on between them, it wasn't for lack of sexual attraction.

"Thanks," she whispered, "but I can't let you pay for the materials, Wyatt."

"Kelly, I..." He hesitated. "I just wanted to help."

"You have." She walked away, more confused and disillusioned than ever.

Everything had been so easy between them at first. She'd loved the laid-back way he flirted with his eyes and teased away her fear. Now his emotions were guarded with her.

Yet he was every bit as protective.

And still the most virile and exciting man she'd ever met.

WYATT STOOD AND WATCHED Kelly walk away. He was a louse, but not near the jerk he'd be if he jumped into a relationship with her only to drag her into his own potential disaster.

The best he could do for her was to make sure she and Jaci were safe until the bastard who had it in for her was behind bars. If Emanuel Leaky was behind this, even that wouldn't be enough.

In the meantime, it was misery being with her and not touching her. And pure hell sleeping a few doors down from her while he ached to have her in his bed.

COLLETTE LOOKED UP from the tomato she was slicing. "I picked these up when I went in for my checkup. They were the best the market had, but these greenhouse varieties only make me long for summer."

"I just long for Tyler to get home," Julie said. "When he gets here, don't expect to see us for at least a week. We're finishing our honeymoon."

They all laughed.

Growing up the only child of a single parent, Kelly was absolutely amazed by how well the Ledgers got along. "Do you always spend this much time together?" she asked, "Or is this because Wyatt's here for a visit?"

"We see a lot of each other," Collette said, "especially on weekends. But we have plenty of privacy, too. We all have our own interests and our own houses."

"It's a very close-knit family," Viviana said as she put the finishing touches on a fruit salad. "I'm thrilled that Briana will grow up in a family like this, even though we will eventually spend part of every week in the city."

Julie reached into the refrigerator for a package of cheese. "It's not that the brothers never argue. They can get into heated discussions on everything from politics to what brand of boots lasts the longest. But if one needs a helping hand, they're all in there together, just like with repairing your house."

Collette set the plate of tomatoes on the table. "If I get any bigger, I won't even be able to reach the table."

"I felt the same way when I was carrying Briana," Viviana said.

"Here's hoping I get back to my normal size as quickly as you did."

"Not to change the subject, but Eve's a brilliant psychiatrist and she has an interesting theory about this family," Julie said.

"What is it?" Kelly asked.

"She feels that Helene and Troy were not only very much in love, but that they created such a strong sense of family that it stayed with their sons through the heartbreak of her murder and Troy's imprisonment, even surviving their years of separation from each other."

"That certainly sounds plausible," Kelly admitted.

"Dylan and I want to create that same sense of family, continuity and love for the land," Collette said. "We want at least four children."

"Don't hesitate to tell me if you think it's none of my business, Kelly, but how long has your husband been dead?" Julie asked.

"Three years."

"You must miss him very much."

"It hasn't been easy." That was true. She'd lost a friend. But not a husband in the truest sense of the word. And definitely not a lover. It was only in the last few days that she was starting to realize how much passion she'd really missed out on in life.

"Was Jaci in kindergarten before you moved to Mustang Run?" Viviana asked.

"No. Things were a bit unsettled in our lives last fall and I decided to hold her back a year." Actually, that decision had been made for her by the FBI, another of the conditions of her witness-protection arrangement. It had seemed the best way to make certain Jaci was safe.

"They say the public schools in this area are excellent," Viviana said.

"If you're interested, our church has a great preschool and kindergarten program that you can enroll her in for the rest of this semester," Julie said.

Out of nowhere, the haunting lullaby from Kelly's nightmare began playing in Kelly's mind.

Stay alive. Stay alive.

"I want to wait until things in our lives have settled down more before I send her off to school every morning."

"There's no hurry," Julie agreed. "She's enjoying the ranch, and the two of you fit into the Ledger family so well."

They might fit, but they weren't—and never would be—part of the family.

And before this was over Wyatt might tear this family apart all over again. Even their early years of closeness might not survive finding out that their father really had murdered their mother.

He's innocent. Helene will tell you.

The one Helene had best talk to was Wyatt.

RUTHANNE PACED THE FLOOR as she punched in Riley's number again. Her head was spinning from that last martini, and she was growing more pissed with every ring of the phone.

Finally, the ringing stopped and she heard a stony hello.

"Where have you been, Riley? I've been trying to reach you for two days."

"You keep forgetting that we're no longer married, Ruthanne. I don't have to account to you for where I've been or whom I've been with."

"Don't take that arrogant tone with me. I *made* you, remember?"

"How could I forget? You reminded me every day for years. What do you want now?"

"We need to talk."

"We have nothing to talk about."

"I think we do. Have you heard that Linda Ann Callister's daughter moved back to town?"

"I've heard. So what?"

"Don't pull that innocent routine with me, Riley. Be here at three o'clock tomorrow. Don't be late."

"And if I don't show up?"

"Then you don't have to worry about Linda Ann's daughter. I'll see that you kiss any chance of being governor goodbye."

FAMILY SINS CAN KILL. *Stay alive. Stay alive.*

Mothers always know. Stay alive. Stay alive.

Hold on tight to love. Stay alive. Kelly, stay alive.

The lullaby grew louder and louder until it became a deafening roar in Kelly's ears. She opened her eyes, but couldn't focus. Ribbons of white moved across the ceiling in slow motion.

The lullaby finally stopped and one of the ribbons drifted featherlike from the air and landed on Kelly's pillow. Kelly reached for it, but the heat from it scorched her hand before she touched it.

A voice wafted across the room, but she couldn't tell where it was coming from. "Talk to your mother, before it's too late."

Kelly picked up the pillow that the ribbon had landed on and hurled it across the room. Reaching for the lamp, she flicked it on and bathed the room in the soothing, subdued light.

Another nightmare. She slid out of the bed and tried

to evict the images from her mind. The lullaby returned to haunt her along with the eerily pleading voice.

Talk to her mother. There was no doubt that finding the engagement picture had inspired her subconscious to concoct that message. Kelly's stress level was clearly off the charts.

She was wide awake now. And thirsty. The nightmares seemed to leave her mouth incredibly dry.

Kelly hadn't bothered to turn on a hall light and she'd stepped into the dark kitchen before she saw the shadowy figure. Her heart slammed against her chest before she realized it was Wyatt sitting at the table in the dark, moonlight slanting across his bare chest.

"You frightened me," she said.

"I'm sorry."

"What are you doing up this time of night?" she asked.

"I couldn't sleep."

"Neither could I." He didn't invite her, but she dropped into the chair opposite his. "We have to talk."

Chapter Thirteen

Wyatt was thankful the lights were off. Even in the glimmer of moonlight shining through the window, the sight of Kelly sitting across from him in her pajamas stirred a hunger so intense, he could barely think.

"You really don't want to hear anything I have to say tonight, Kelly. It's gruesome and depressing."

"Try me," she whispered. "What is keeping you awake?"

"The same thing that's kept me awake since I was thirteen."

"The question of who murdered your mother?"

"Right, but it has added implications now. If I do find out it's my father, that is going to destroy this whole family. If I don't find out who killed my mother, I am never going to be able to live with myself. It's a no-win situation."

"Unless you find out that Troy is innocent. You surely haven't ruled that out."

"No, but I don't see anything in what he's said or shown me that's negated what was presented at the trial."

"Tell me about the trial."

"Are you looking for nightmare material?"

"No, I have a stalker to provide that."

"The basic case the prosecution presented was that Mother was leaving Troy. He came home from lunch, found her with her bags packed and shot her three times."

"Why was she leaving him?"

"According to the testimony of her best friend, Mother had said just that morning she'd had enough and was going to put an end to the strife. That's not verbatim."

"What about the boys?"

"According to the witness, she was coming back for us and leaving our father completely alone."

"Did only one friend attest to that?"

"Yes, but several other friends testified that Mother's parents were always trying to get her to leave Troy. Apparently they thought Mother had married beneath her."

"Were you that poor?"

"If my parents were struggling with financial issues, I never knew it. I mean, we didn't go to Disney World on vacation or spend Christmas skiing in Colorado, but neither did most of the other ranchers' kids. I don't remember ever wanting for anything."

"What evidence did your father's defense team provide?"

"Basically nothing. They couldn't dispute that Mother was killed with Troy's gun. They couldn't come up with another viable suspect. And Troy did nothing to help his case. According to news reports at the time, he sat there day after day showing a complete lack of emotion.

"The only exception was when they showed the pictures of the crime scene and talked about his five young sons being left without a mother. The prosecutor used that outbreak of weeping in his closing statement, saying that the guilt finally got to Troy."

"Maybe he was hurting so deeply that he couldn't face the trial and had to shut it out until the photographs made the pain too much to bear."

"I hope you're right. But I still need facts and the only way I'm going to prove Troy didn't do it is to prove someone else did."

He pushed his hands against his temples like a vise, trying to ease a nagging headache that had hammered away at him all day. "Now aren't you sorry you asked?"

"No."

"Let's talk about you," he said, though he wasn't sure he could take hearing about a superhero husband to whom no other man could ever compare.

"What about me?"

"How long were you married before your husband died?"

"Two years. He died of a fast-growing malignancy in his stomach."

"I'm sorry. You must have been devastated."

"I was. He was a wonderful person, kind and intelligent and a good father."

She'd made no mention of passion, yet Wyatt knew from one kiss that she was anything but cold.

"How did you meet him?"

"Unlike my mother, I was not the scholarly type. I dropped out of college after my sophomore year and spent two years wandering Europe. That's when I fell in love with jewelry design and when I met Adolph."

Adolph. Try to compete with that, cowboy cop.

"He was twenty years older than me, and far more sophisticated. I was intrigued by him and infatuated with his knowledge of all the fine arts."

"Even though he was old enough to be your father?"

"I'd never known a father, so I never gave the father aspect of it a thought. We started having coffee together. One thing led to another and one night we took it all the way—at my insistence, I should add. I was frustrated by his lack of physical response to me."

"That's difficult to imagine."

"Is it, Wyatt? I seem to inspire that same reluctance on your part. Anyway, I got pregnant in spite of using protection. I know that's rare, but it happens. He asked me to marry him and I accepted."

"Did you love him?"

"I thought I did at the time. I respected him. He was a fascinating conversationalist. He was honorable and thoughtful and he encouraged me to explore my interest in jewelry design."

"You forgot to mention love."

"Adolph came out of the closet a year later."

"That explains a lot. But you stayed married?"

"The cancer had been diagnosed by then. He needed me."

Wyatt reached across the table and placed his hands on top of hers. It was meant to be just a comforting touch, but his body reacted as if she'd just stripped naked in front of him. He pushed away from the table. "We should try to get some sleep," he said, his voice so husky with desire, he couldn't even recognize it.

"One more question, Wyatt."

"Shoot."

"Why kiss me senseless and then pull away as if you can't bear to touch me? Why avoid being alone with me or even making eye contact? I haven't changed."

"I'm just following the lawman's code. A cop never gets personally involved with a woman he's protecting.

It makes him lose his edge and become more susceptible to making mistakes."

She stood and glared down at him. "That's bull and you know it. You're afraid of me, Wyatt. Afraid that you might fall hard for me and that I might interfere with your burning desire to settle a score for your mother no matter who it hurts."

"You're reading this all wrong."

"I don't think so, Wyatt. You may be a big, tough cop, but you're afraid of facing your own emotions head-on. I may have married a man I didn't love, but I've never run from love the way you do."

He stood and backed away from the table. "Fear has nothing to do with this."

"Prove it."

She walked over and stopped right in front of him, so close he could feel her breath on his bare chest.

"Kiss me right now and prove you're not afraid." She took his right hand in hers and pressed it to her breast so that he could feel the peak of her nipple beneath her cotton pajamas.

He lost it then and he kissed her hard, ravaging her lips, exploding in a rush of desire he couldn't have stopped if he wanted to. He didn't want to.

So he picked her up and carried her to his bed.

Chapter Fourteen

Kelly's heart was racing as Wyatt ripped a multicolored quilt from the bed and laid her on top of a crisp white sheet. The linens smelled of Wyatt, a mixture of soap and pine and musk. There was little time to revel in the intoxication of the scents as he stretched out beside her and kissed her until her lungs begged for air.

He kissed her eyes, her nose, her cheeks before he finally let his lips return to her mouth. When his fingers fumbled too long on the buttons of her pajama top, she helped him, wishing he'd just rip it off and take her savagely.

Once her breasts were freed, he cupped them in his hands and sucked her nipples, nibbling and pinching lightly so that they pebbled and peaked as she arched toward him.

Her hands roamed his broad shoulders, as his fingers created deliciously heated spirals of pleasure across her abdomen. And then he dipped his fingers beneath the elastic waistband of her pajamas and the hunger she'd kept famished too long exploded inside her.

She trembled as he kissed the column of her neck and put his mouth to her ear. "Are you sure you want this, Kelly? If you don't, or if you think you'll face to-morrow with regrets, tell me now."

"I want you, Wyatt. I'm sure I want you. Just you. No promises you can't keep. No commitments you can't honor. Just one night where I can feel and love and let go without inhibition."

One night of heaven with no thoughts of Emanuel Leaky or thugs or threatening texts. No thoughts of anything but Wyatt and the way he protected and thrilled and was setting her heart and soul on fire.

She wiggled out of her pajama bottoms while Wyatt shucked off his jeans. She consumed him with her eyes as he stretched out naked beside her. He might not ever be hers to keep, but nothing would ever take this moment from her.

He straddled her and she wrapped her legs around him as he thrust the hard length of his erection deep inside her. He thrust again and again and she writhed beneath him until a volcano of hot, wet desire erupted inside her. He exploded with her in an orgasm so intense that a sob tore from her throat.

Wyatt rolled off her and cradled her in his arms. "Did I hurt you?"

"No. It's just been so long, and making love with you felt so right."

"I don't ever want to hurt you, Kelly. It will kill me if I do, but…"

She kissed his words away. "I told you I'm not asking for promises of forever."

"I was just going to say that I'm through fighting what I feel for you. If you want to get rid of me now you'll have to kick me out of your life, and I'm not even sure that would do it."

"In that case, you'll be around for a long, long time."

Unless a madman and an almost twenty-year-old murder destroyed them both.

WHEN SHE HADN'T HEARD from Sheriff McGuire about the fingerprint check by noon the next day, Kelly grew antsy. If Viviana and Briana hadn't come to the house to keep her company, she'd have been climbing the walls by now.

Making love with Wyatt had definitely changed her mind about looking for an apartment, but it made her no less concerned about the danger that kept threading its way through her life.

"Why don't we drive into town and check the guys' progress on the house," Viviana said. "We might even be able to talk them into taking a lunch break with us."

"That's a great idea," Kelly said. "I'll go find Troy and see if he wants to go with us."

"I'm sure he does," Viviana said. "No doubt it's killing him to be left out of the construction fun and the chance to spend more time with Wyatt."

"Did the heart attack last year limit his physical activities?" Kelly asked.

"Somewhat. But he's here today because he drew bodyguard duty. Didn't Wyatt tell you?"

"No." For some stupid reason she'd felt so safe at the ranch she hadn't even thought the perp, as Wyatt called him, might show up here. "Then we should stay here on the ranch," Kelly said. "We can't leave Julie and Collette alone."

"Well, you're never really alone on the ranch. Dylan just hired two new wranglers and that brings the number up to six. But Collette and Julie aren't on the ranch today anyway. They went into Austin to pick up a lamp Collette ordered for the nursery."

"How long will that take?"

"At least a couple of hours, but then they're stopping by Sean's so Collette can go with him to look at a stallion he's thinking of buying as a stud horse. They won't be home until close to dinnertime."

"And you got stuck here with me?"

"Not true. I went horseback riding before Dakota left and then came home and finished a book I was reading. See, we do all pursue our own interests."

In minutes they were loaded into Troy's truck. Viviana squeezed in between Briana and Jaci who were safely buckled in their respective car and booster seats. Briana kicked and fussed until the car started. Then she happily entertained them with her delightful mix of recognizable and unrecognizable syllables for the remainder of the ride.

Jaci excitedly talked of going on the horseback ride Wyatt had promised over breakfast this morning. His effort to get to know Jaci had both surprised and pleased Kelly. She was glad they were going to town. He'd only been gone a few hours, but she couldn't wait to see him again.

The first person she saw when they pulled into the driveway of her house was Sheriff McGuire. He and Wyatt were near the spot where the fallen tree had once stood.

"You go ahead and get whatever news the sheriff's delivering," Troy said. "I'll watch Jaci."

"Thanks."

"We have an ID," the sheriff said as soon as she walked up.

"Who? Does he live in Mustang Run? Do you know where to find him?"

"I think we'd best find a more private place before

I start answering those questions you're throwing out like a shiny-suited lawyer."

"It's cool enough we can sit in my truck if we leave the doors open," Wyatt said.

Neither of them indicated by their tone or expressions that this was good news. The anxiety hit her all over again.

"Like I just told Wyatt, the man who stole your car and the Corvette is Jerome Hurley."

Wyatt already knew what the sheriff had to say. But Wyatt was way ahead of him. He knew why Jerome was targeting Kelly and he knew that Emanuel was behind it. All he needed was proof.

Wyatt had told Kelly from the beginning that his promise to keep secret her involvement with Leaky would cease to be binding if he found out that association had put her in danger.

He was convinced now that it had. He wasn't convinced that sharing that information with the sheriff was the best move. Wyatt trusted his own instincts and experience. He'd stop Hurley, dead or alive. Right now he didn't much care which. He turned his attention back to the conversation between McGuire and Kelly.

"He was convicted of raping a Mustang Run rancher's wife fourteen years ago," McGuire explained. "He's only been out of prison for two months. The probation officer has already lost track of him, and it blows me up like a toad that nobody told me about that."

"Do you have any idea where to start looking for him?" Kelly asked.

"His mother's dead. His dad is in jail, so there's no checking with either of them. But we'll contact any of his old friends that we can locate, and we're checking all the spots where the county's lowlife usually hangs out."

The sheriff turned toward the backseat. "Did I cover everything with Kelly I covered with you and Dakota, Wyatt?"

"I think so."

"This man's dangerous, Kelly. We can assume he's the one who broke into your house the other night and sent you that text. We just don't have proof of that yet.

"If you didn't have the Ledgers looking after you, I'd see about putting you in some kind of protective custody until we arrest Hurley. But I can't give you any better men to protect you than you already have."

"I realize that," Kelly said.

"If he shows his face anywhere in this county, we'll arrest him," McGuire said. "And I've notified every other county in the state, as well as the state troopers to be on the lookout for him, too."

"I guess that's all you can do," Kelly said.

But it wasn't all Wyatt could do. He was no longer a cop. The rules of warrants and illegal searches and questioning people without just cause didn't apply to him. He'd start today, combing the area that Hurley could have walked to the night he left Kelly's car in her driveway.

"At least he knows who to search for now," Kelly said as McGuire drove away.

"That's a start," Wyatt agreed. He slipped his arm around her waist as they walked back toward the house. He considered telling her that he was almost certain that this was tied in to Emanuel Leaky, but there was no reason to frighten her any more than she already was. Not yet, anyway.

"I'm glad we arrived when we did," Kelly said, "but

we actually stopped by to see if you and your brothers want to go to lunch with us."

"Dakota drove to the nearest fast-food joint and picked up Cokes and burgers about an hour ago."

But he did want to talk to Troy alone before they left.

Wyatt cornered Troy while Kelly was talking about damage and repairs with Dylan. Dakota and Viviana had gone outside with the children.

"Dakota told me that Jerome Hurley is behind this," Troy said. "He was bad enough before he went to prison. Looks like he came out of the slammer even more rotten. I wouldn't put anything past him."

"I agree. I have something I have to do for the next few hours. I'd appreciate it if you'd keep an extra close watch on Kelly and Jaci until I get home."

"I'd planned to do that without you asking."

"Going to lunch is fine as long as there are people around. It will take her mind off things. I'll be back at the ranch before dark. If there's trouble…"

"I know what to do if there's trouble. Take care of the man causing it. I'd like nothing better."

"I don't expect trouble at the ranch. This guy isn't looking for a fight. He wants to catch Kelly alone." And leave no witnesses.

"And this is what you like about law enforcement?" Troy asked.

"No, but catching the bad guys makes it all worthwhile."

IT WAS NEARLY TWO in the afternoon when they finally made it to Abby's Diner. Kelly was glad they were running late. With the lunch crowd having thinned out, it would be easier for her to grab a few minutes alone with Abby.

Even with Kelly's current crisis gearing up for a possible arrest, she couldn't get her mother's decades-old engagement picture out of her mind. The latest nightmare wasn't helping.

She wouldn't pry for gossip about her mother. But the engagement had been announced in the newspaper so it wasn't a deep, dark secret. All Kelly wanted from Abby was the intended groom's name.

The name of the man who could possibly be her biological father.

On second thought, maybe she should just leave the past in the past.

The same hostess met them at the door, but without the extra sway to her hips or the flirtatious smile she'd had for Wyatt. The restaurant was less crowded but more noisy. All of the activity seemed to center on one of the back tables.

"Who's the celebrity hidden by the fawning crowd?" Troy asked as they were seated in a window booth.

"Senator Foley. We weren't expecting him. He just showed up. Can you imagine the man who may be the next governor of Texas just showing up at Abby's Diner? Abby's not impressed. She hasn't even bothered to come out of the kitchen to talk to him."

"Abby's known him since long before he was a senator," Troy said. "And it takes a lot to impress her."

Once the hostess left, Kelly craned her neck for a better view but still couldn't see the senator through the crowd. "My mother was on his staff for his very first campaign," she told Viviana.

"You should go talk to him," Viviana said.

"I'm sure he wouldn't remember me and maybe not my mother. That was twenty years ago, or close to it.

Besides I didn't get a very warm reception from his ex-wife when I met her in the horse barn."

"That's just Ruthanne," Troy said. "The senator will give you a warm greeting whether he remembers you or not. He's looking for votes."

The waitress came with their drinks and after she took their orders, Kelly stood up from the table.

"If you don't mind, I think I'll go over and say hello while we're waiting for our food," Kelly said. "Jaci, do you want to go with me to meet Senator Foley?"

Jaci twisted her mouth in a bizarre shape. Briana laughed out loud. "I'll stay here. Briana likes my faces."

"Okay. I'll be right back."

She anticipated having to inch her way past a crowd of people to get close enough to get his attention. But he saw her approach and stood to greet her. Well, not greet her exactly, but openly stare. Not particularly politician cool.

She extended a hand. "I'm Kelly Burger. I know you don't remember me, but I met you years ago when my mother was on your very first campaign staff."

"Linda Ann Callister."

"Yes, but how did you know that's who I was talking about?"

"You look so much like her I did a double take when I saw you. Sit down," he said, motioning to the empty chair kitty-corner to his. "It was great talking to all of you," he said to the crowd around him, "but I haven't seen this young lady in a very long time and we have some catching up to do."

"I can only stay a few minutes," Kelly said. "I'm having lunch with friends and they're watching my daughter while I came over to say hello."

"Which one is your daughter?"

"The one making faces." Kelly pointed her out. "Her name is Jaci."

"She has the Callister good looks, as well."

"Thank you."

"How is Linda Ann?" he asked.

"She's doing great. She recently retired from her position as dean of a small women's college in the Northeast and she and her husband have moved back to Texas."

"Where in Texas?"

"Plano."

"Then she's happy?"

"I think so."

"Would you tell her I said hello the next time you see her?"

"I'll be certain to."

"Tell her I still think of her often and that the ridiculous statue she won at the State Fair still sits on my desk."

"I will."

"How does she feel about your moving back to Mustang Run?"

"She doesn't know yet. I thought I'd surprise her after the move was made and I'm settled in enough to insist she come for a visit. How did you know I was moving back?"

"Word gets around."

"Ah, yes. Small-town news distribution. The thing Mother disliked most about Mustang Run." She glanced back to check on Jaci. "They've served our food, so I'd best go eat before it gets cold."

He stood with her, took her hand and held it for a tad too long. "Thanks for stopping by. It meant more than you know."

He had seemed glad to see her, almost too glad. And he remembered her mother extremely well, right down to the cheap prize she'd won at a fair that he still kept on his desk.

Kelly wondered exactly what had gone on between him and her mother during the time she worked for him. She suspected that it went beyond a typical employee/employer relationship.

No wonder Ruthanne had taken an instant dislike to her.

Kelly was beginning to think she didn't know her mother at all. But she wouldn't bother Abby with her question about the broken engagement. The answers should come directly from the source.

RILEY WATCHED KELLY walk away, amazed at how much she looked like her mother. She had the sway to her hips. Classy, yet subtly seductive. Back straight. Head high. An air about her that snared men's attention and didn't let go.

Even her nose was the same, tilted just enough to make her appear beguiling, yet mischievous. Perhaps the most striking feature they shared were the full, soft lips that had once driven Riley mad with desire.

If he'd ever truly loved anyone in his life, it was Linda Ann.

That was a lifetime ago. He'd been a nobody then. Now he was rising to the top like cream—or like a dead fish. Next stop, the governor's mansion. And then, if he played his cards right, it could be on to the White House.

Reason enough that his past had to stay buried. People these days might forgive a politician an indiscretion or two, but some things would never be forgiven.

He'd passed that line almost twenty years ago.

WYATT GRABBED his work-worn Stetson from a hook near the back door, stomped down the back steps and strode toward the woodshed. They weren't short of logs for the fireplace, but he needed the release of swinging an ax.

He'd gotten nowhere that afternoon. If anyone he'd questioned had seen Hurley since his release, they'd done a good job of lying. And Wyatt could usually detect a liar before the words left their mouth. It was in their eyes, their expression, even the movement of their Adam's apple.

He picked up the ax and began to swing, furiously splitting logs until sweat began to pour down his forehead and into his eyes. He buried the point of the ax into a log and stopped to yank his black T-shirt over his head. Wadded, the shirt made the perfect handkerchief for wiping his brow.

The temperature had climbed to seventy today. Two days from now a new cold front was expected, this one bringing a slight chance of snow. Even for the Texas Hill Country, the weather this January seemed out of sync.

Wyatt remembered going horseback riding with Troy one year when a light snow was falling. They'd ridden to the bluff on the far northern end of the spread and found a deer that had gotten tangled in the limbs of a downed mesquite tree. Wyatt had helped free the frightened doe.

When they'd returned to the house, he'd heard Troy tell his mother what a fine man Wyatt was becoming.

That was before everything had fallen apart.

When it had, Wyatt hadn't been a man at all. He'd tried to keep his brothers together, had begged and finally cried when his grandparents had separated them and farmed them out to any relative who'd take them. When his brothers had needed him most, he'd had no power to help.

And now he was here on a mission that might destroy their lives all over again.

But he was beginning to see why his brothers believed in Troy's innocence. Wyatt had to admit that Troy's research was much more detailed and comprehensive than he'd expected.

But even if he bought into Troy's innocence for the sake of argument, Wyatt didn't buy into Troy's random murder scenario, at least not yet.

Wyatt heard footsteps and looked up to see Kelly walking toward him. The late afternoon sun turned her hair the color of a strawberry field. When she smiled and waved, he almost choked on the desire that swelled inside him and the ache from knowing there was almost no way this relationship could ever work out.

She was infatuated with her protector the same way she'd been infatuated with her husband before she'd married him. She saw in Wyatt only what she wanted to see, instead of the hard-edged cop he'd become. He'd be a damn poor catch as a husband.

He picked up the ax and swung as hard as he could to release the fury and frustration that burned in his gut.

KELLY STOOD FOR A MOMENT, watching the flex and release of Wyatt's muscles as he wielded the ax. When he buried the blade of the ax, she stepped into his arms, relishing the thrill of his kiss before she backed away.

She splayed the palms of her hands across his chest. "You are the most gorgeously virile cowboy I have ever slept with."

"You need to get around more."

"No, I'm happy right here."

"But you know I'm not really a cowboy," Wyatt said.

"You walk like one, talk like one, look like one and you sure fit in well on Willow Creek Ranch."

"I have to admit I like the pace of this lifestyle—but only to a point."

"You can't miss being a cop. You still are one, just without the badge. I know you spent the afternoon attempting to track down Jerome Hurley. And you're driven to find your mother's killer."

"True, but what would I do with myself once they're behind bars?"

"Sheriff McGuire appears to stay busy. Not that I'm trying to get you to change your lifestyle."

"Troy tells me you had a chat with Riley Foley today," Wyatt said.

"I did. I was surprised at how well he remembered my mother after all those years."

"When was it you said she worked for him?"

"Nineteen years ago."

"The same year my mother was killed. Riley had already been elected and had taken office when his wife testified at Troy's trial."

"Was she a character witness?"

"She was my mother's best friend who I told you gave damaging testimony against my father."

"That's surprising."

"Why?"

"When I met her in the horse barn, she was coming

on strong to Troy and acting very possessive in case I had any ideas of moving in on her territory."

"According to my brothers, she's been trying to snare Troy ever since he was released from prison. They say he's not interested."

"Released, but on a technicality," Kelly said, thinking out loud. "Kind of odd for her to be making a play for a man that her testimony helped send to prison for killing his wife."

"It doesn't make a lot of sense, does it?"

"No." But neither Ruthanne nor the senator were the reason she'd come looking for Wyatt. "I'm thinking of driving up to Plano to visit my mother tomorrow. I've already talked to Julie. She's agreed to watch Jaci for me and to let me use her car. It's only a three-hour drive. I'll be back long before dark."

"I thought you said you didn't want to worry her."

"I don't plan to mention Jerome Hurley or even that my car was stolen. I found something in one of the boxes Grams left for me that I need to ask her about."

"Do you want to talk to me about it?"

"I wouldn't mind getting your take on it."

"Fire away."

Kelly explained the engagement announcement and the significance of the date. She didn't mention the nightmare or the lullaby that wouldn't let go of her.

"Don't you think this can wait until Jerome is arrested?"

"I can't explain this in any way that makes sense, but I feel that I have to talk to Mother now."

"In that case, I'm going with you."

She never doubted for a minute that he would.

JEROME REACHED for his phone on the first ring. "Hello."

"I'm ready to talk terms, but not on the phone."

"Name the time and place and bring cash."

"Are you sure your phone is untraceable?"

"Do you think I plan to go back to that hellhole prison?"

"Then I'll meet you at midnight on the cutoff road near Dowman-Lagoste Bridge."

"I know the spot well." He'd dropped off a body there once. As far as he knew what was left of it was still sleeping with the fishes.

He broke the connection. The deal was a go. The same deal he'd made to kill Helene Ledger almost twenty years ago. Only the victim had changed.

And the payout.

Chapter Fifteen

The house in Plano was a single-level brick on a quiet cul-de-sac. The yard was meticulous with expertly trimmed hedges and weedless flower beds. Kelly had no doubt that they'd find the same classic style and understated perfection inside.

Linda Ann lived a meticulous life, following inflexible schedules that left room for little spontaneity. Kelly had never doubted for a second that her mother loved her. Linda Ann just had trouble with warmth and expressing emotion.

Yet, she'd obviously been provocative enough that Senator Foley had never forgotten her.

Kelly pushed the doorbell. Seconds later, her mother appeared at the door, apparently already dressed for her early afternoon class. They exchanged a quick hug and then Kelly introduced Wyatt as Wyatt Alan, using his middle name for his last at Wyatt's insistence.

In case Linda Ann remembered his parents from her years in Mustang Run, Wyatt did not want to hijack Kelly's concerns with talk of his mother's murder and his father's release from prison.

"I'm delighted to meet you, Wyatt. I'm sorry Walter isn't here to join us, but my husband is out of the country for a few weeks, teaching a seminar at the University of London."

"I'm sorry we missed him," Kelly said. A white lie. She couldn't have asked the questions she needed answered in front of him. This way she didn't have to hurt his feelings by kicking him out of the room.

They followed Linda Ann to the living room.

"I wish Jaci could have come with you," Linda Ann said. "It seems forever since I've seen her."

"I'll bring her up soon. But like I told you on the phone, this is just a quick trip."

"Yes, you said you had something important to discuss with me. I worried all night. Does this concern your health? If there's something wrong, I want you to level with me, Kelly."

"It's not my health, Mom. I'm fine. I just have some things I'd like to talk to you about."

"Thank goodness. You've kept so to yourself this past year, I feared you were hiding something from me."

Only a year in protective custody.

"I have blueberry scones. Would you like to have them with coffee as we talk or would you rather wait until we've finished the discussion?"

"Let's talk first," Kelly said, growing more nervous by the second.

"I'm moving back to Mustang Run, Mom."

Linda Ann sat up even straighter, clasping her hands in her lap as if she needed something to hold on to. "Why would you move there?" she asked. "You'll be limiting your opportunities. Why not Santa Fe, or Carmel or even Austin where creativity is nourished?"

"I'm moving into Grams's house. I'll be able to work at home and spend more time with Jaci. I've contacted several jewelers in Austin and San Antonio and they've expressed an interest in carrying my work."

"It sounds as if you've made up your mind. I wish we could have discussed this first."

Kelly reached into her handbag and pulled out the brown envelope containing the engagement announcement. She leaned over and handed it to her mother.

"I found this in a box of Grams's photos."

Linda Ann pulled out the clipping and stared at the picture. "I can't believe your grandmother saved this. Surely you didn't come all the way to Plano to talk about a broken engagement in my distant past."

It did sound a bit foolish now that Kelly was here. She should never have let the nightmares get to her. But she was here now. She might as well ask her questions.

"You never mentioned being engaged before you met my father."

"It wasn't worth mentioning. It was a mistake that we righted before the wedding."

"The date is on the picture, Mom. That's seven months before the date on my birth certificate."

Linda Ann closed her eyes. When she opened them again, her face was strained and she rubbed a spot on her hand as if she were trying to remove a stain.

"Were you pregnant by the man you were engaged to…"

"Or was I cheating on him with your father?" Linda Ann asked, finishing the question for her.

"I'm not judging you, Mom. You know what a mess my marriage was. I just need to know if my biological father is still alive. I'm grown. There is no use for secrets between us."

Linda Ann stood and paced the room, the first time

Kelly ever remembered seeing her when she wasn't in complete control.

"You're right, Kelly. It's time you know the truth and I'm tired of living with the lies. But you have to remember that we're talking about a very short period of my life thirty years ago."

"I realize that."

"I was engaged to Riley Foley, big man on campus. Not the brainiest, not a varsity athlete, not even rich. But he had charisma."

As he still did, Kelly thought. It had taken him far in politics.

"We started dating our senior year and he asked me to marry him at Christmas. Your grandmother was far from rich, but she wanted me to have a nice wedding so she spent a chunk of Dad's insurance money on the wedding, money she should have kept to live on."

"That sounds like Grams. Generous to a fault."

"The wedding was all planned and for the most part paid for. Two weeks before the wedding, Riley broke off the engagement. He said he was in love with someone else."

"Ruthanne?"

"None other. Daughter of one of Mustang Run's richest citizens. Her father owned major interest in an oil company and one of the largest ranches in the area. I was furious with him, hurt for Grams who'd wasted so much money, and embarrassed for myself for being dumped practically at the altar."

Kelly's stomach rolled as the truth became clear. "So Senator Foley is my father?"

"Yes, but I never told him. I left town and started a new life. I had your grandmother spread the news that I'd met a marvelous man and then later that he'd died before we could get married. I told everyone that I was pregnant and thrilled to be carrying his baby. It sounds juvenile and stupid now, but it was my way of coping."

"Did Grams know the truth?"

"Yes, but she never told a soul."

"In spite of all that, you went to work for Riley Foley ten years later?"

"Yes, a decision I'll regret for as long as I live. I ran into him at a hotel in Boston where we were attending different conventions. We had a few drinks. He told me how bad his marriage was and that he had never stopped loving me."

And her mother—whom Kelly had always thought of as being the most together person she knew—had been insecure enough to buy into that.

"Riley persuaded me to give up my professorship in political science and run his campaign. We spent the rest of that week in Boston together, blowing off our respective conventions except for the one paper I had to present."

"Ruthanne must have loved hearing that you were working with her husband."

"She was livid and figured out quickly that we were having an affair. But it was Helene Ledger who actually caught us in the act."

At the mention of Helene's name, Wyatt's whole demeanor changed. He sat straighter and his gaze bored into Linda Ann.

"Did you say that Helene Ledger discovered that you and Riley were having an affair?"

"Yes. She'd stopped by campaign headquarters to discuss volunteering. She saw Riley and I kiss outside the office building and then she followed us to a hotel."

"How long was this before she was murdered?" Wyatt asked.

Linda Ann stared him down. "I'm getting to that."

But Wyatt was all detective now. Kelly saw the rugged determination in his eyes and in the set of his jaw. This new edginess made her nervous. This was her mother they were talking to, not one of his murder suspects.

"Helene went to Riley and told him that if he didn't tell Ruthanne the truth, she would."

"And did she?" Wyatt questioned.

"I don't know. I only know that Riley believed she would, but he said he didn't care. He loved me and he was going to leave Ruthanne and marry me even if it cost him the race for representative. I'd decided it was time to tell him he had a daughter, but then I never got the chance."

Wyatt leaned forward, his gaze riveted to Linda Ann. "What stopped you?"

"Before I saw him again, Helene was murdered. I went into hysteria. I called Riley and accused him of killing her. He swore to me he had nothing to do with the murder."

"Did you believe him?" Wyatt asked.

"I did after I calmed down. Riley may not be a faithful husband or fiancé for that matter, but he's not a killer."

"What happened next?" Wyatt asked. "Did you continue to see Foley?"

"No. I finally came to my senses. I wanted nothing to do with Riley or his campaign. I resigned from his staff and moved back to Boston."

"Did you call the police after Helene's death and explain her threat to expose your affair?"

"No, I should have, I know, but that would have made them go after Riley and I knew he was innocent. It might have even ruined his chances of ever having a career in politics. And, I hate to admit this, but I was still in love with him."

"When was the next time you saw him?"

"I haven't to this day. I've seen him on television at times when something he does politically makes the national news. But I vowed then that I would never get involved with him again."

Kelly fought an onslaught of vertigo and nausea. She'd come here seeking the truth, but she'd never expected to hear anything this morbid and repulsive. Still, she felt for her mother having to live with the sordid secrets. No wonder she'd poured her energy into her work. Her personal life was such a horrid mess.

"I cried with relief when Troy Ledger was arrested and again when he was convicted of the murder," Linda Ann admitted. "I was thankful to know that Helene Ledger's murder had nothing to do with her threatening to expose my affair with Riley. I'd like to think that if they hadn't found Helene's killer, I'd have spoken up. Sadly, I'm not sure that I would have.

"It was the horrible end of a sickening chapter in my life. I decided then that I would never allow my daughter to become a pawn for Riley to play against me."

"So you decided to let me go on indefinitely believing my father was dead."

"I did. If I made a mistake, it was out of love and the fear that you'd pay for my sins."

Family sins can kill. Stay alive. Stay alive.

The lullaby echoed through her mind again. It was as if the nightmare had been trying to warn her of this.

The nightmare or Helene's spirit. Only, Kelly didn't believe in ghosts.

Tears rolled down her mother's face. "I'm so sorry that you had to find out about your father this way, Kelly. Can you ever forgive me for choosing to live a lie and to make you live it, as well?"

Kelly walked over and gave her mother a hug. "I told you I'm not here to judge. You're my mother and I love you. But I'm glad you finally told me the truth."

They didn't stay for scones and coffee. Kelly was sure her stomach wouldn't tolerate food.

Five minutes later, they were in Wyatt's truck and on their way back to Mustang Run. The full truth of what she'd learned began to sink in.

Riley Foley was her father no matter that her mother was convinced otherwise, and there was a chance that he, and not Troy, was behind Helene's murder. She understood better now why Wyatt was determined to find out the truth about his father.

Only it was much worse for Wyatt than for her. He'd known and loved his father. The senator was a stranger who'd donated his sperm before breaking her mother's heart.

And the brutally murdered victim had been Wyatt's mother.

Kelly reached over and rested her hand on Wyatt's thigh. "I'm afraid to even think about what comes next."

"Do you want to go and confront the senator?"

"Maybe one day. Not yet."

"You do realize that if I discover that he murdered my mother, I'll do everything I can to make sure he's arrested and convicted?"

"I assumed that you would."

Wyatt would be investigating her biological father as a primary suspect in the murder of his mother because of an affair he had with her mother. It couldn't get much more complicated than this.

How would they ever maintain a relationship with that hanging over them? And even if they made it through that, Wyatt had given no indication that he planned to stay in Mustang Run or take her with him when he left.

They had only here and now.

"There is one other thing I should tell you," Wyatt said.

She didn't like the seriousness of his tone. "Is this something I want to hear?"

"No, but I think it's only fair I tell you that I'm convinced Jerome is a paid assassin hired by someone working on Emanuel Leaky's behalf. And it isn't a wild theory. I have solid reasons to back it up."

And if Emanuel Leaky knew she was behind his arrest, then her only option was going back into witness protection with Jaci.

Would this never end?

TWO DAYS LATER, things appeared to be at a standstill in the search for Jerome Hurley, though they were moving at a dizzying pace in every other area of Kelly's life.

First and foremost in Kelly's mind, the tension between Wyatt and his father had greatly diminished now that Wyatt had an evidential reason to hold out hope of his father's innocence. Armed with the information of the affair, he had a new focus for his investigation into Helene's murder.

Sheriff McGuire had deputized Wyatt on a temporary basis so that if he did find Jerome Hurley, he could arrest him. Wyatt was determined to do just that. He hit the streets every day and sometimes well into the night searching for him or any clue as to his whereabouts.

When Kelly had voiced the possibility that Jerome had moved on, Wyatt had delivered a brusque reminder that thinking like that could get her killed. He was convinced that Leaky had put out a hit on her and Jerome had accepted the task. Now he was merely waiting for opportunity.

Dylan, Dakota and Sean had torn out all the wet and damaged carpet, Sheetrock and wood in her house and had hired a roofing company to install a new roof the next week. She didn't have the heart to tell them or face the reality herself that even when Jerome was arrested, she might never be able to move into her house.

Not if Emanuel Leaky wanted her dead.

Finally, she had her car back from the sheriff, though Wyatt had ordered her to never leave the ranch alone. She had certainly disrupted the Ledger household.

She made herself a cup of hot tea and then went back to the family room where Jaci was playing dress up and clomping around the room in a pair of Kelly's high heels and a skirt with an elastic waist that she wore as a dress. An old purse that Viviana had given her completed the ensemble.

"I'm going to town to buy diapers for my babies," Jaci said.

"Babies need diapers," Kelly agreed.

"I'll buy them some candy, too."

"I don't think candy is good for babies."

"Uh-huh. My babies like it."

"So does mine."

The doorbell rang. Jaci ran to greet the company whoever it might be. "Let me get the door," Kelly said.

She put her eye to the peephole and then unlocked the dead bolt and swung it open to Collette and Dylan.

"I didn't know you already had company," Dylan said, smiling at Jaci. "Who is this lovely lady?"

"It's me." Jaci giggled and then dropped her handbag to hug them both.

"We're driving over to Sean's and since we didn't see Wyatt's truck around, we thought you and Jaci might like to go with us," Collette said.

"Isn't it late to be driving to Bandera?"

"It's only a few minutes after two," Collette said. "We'll be there by three-thirty, have dinner, visit and be home again before nine."

"Can we please, Momma? Please," Jaci pleaded. "I want to play with Joey."

"And Collette is going stir crazy since she can't take those afternoon rides to exercise the horses," Dylan said.

Kelly was growing a bit stir crazy herself. Jerome Hurley was making a prisoner of her. "We'd love to go," Kelly said. "I'll get our jackets and tell Troy we're leaving. Shall I ask him if he wants to go?"

"I asked him earlier this morning," Dylan said. "He said no. I think he's buried in those charts back in his bedroom again."

"You and Dylan can talk about the remodeling job on your house on the drive over," Collette said. "He has a fabulous idea for tearing out that wall that separates your kitchen from the living room and making that one big open area."

"We can raise that ceiling, too," Dylan said, "and put windows across the side so you get more natural light. I drew up some plans, but I left them in your house. Next time you're there, take a look at them."

"You guys are amazing. I can't wait to see what you've come up with."

She'd started toward the back of the house when she heard the door open again. When she heard Wyatt's voice, all thought of leaving with Dylan and Collette evaporated. Hopefully, they'd still take Jaci along. Time alone with Wyatt was at a premium.

WYATT ATTACHED Jaci's booster seat to the backseat of Dylan's truck and then double-checked to make sure it was secure. He was still awkward with Jaci. He hadn't spent much time around kids since he'd been one himself.

But she'd stolen his heart, and he was making progress with her. He'd do better at it once his total focus didn't have to be finding Jerome Hurley. Even finding his mother's killer had temporarily taken a backseat to the new sense of urgency.

Once he knew Kelly was safe, he'd have to make decisions about his and Kelly's relationship. He was absolutely mad about her. She appeared to feel the same about him. But the complications had increased dramatically over the past few days.

How would she feel when he was forced to expose to the media her mother's long-buried secrets? How would she feel if his investigation destroyed her biological father while clearing the name of his?

"Feel free to jot notes on those drawings I left at the house," Dylan said. "We're just at the idea stage, so encourage Kelly to offer hers, too."

"Will do."

Jaci crawled into her booster seat while Collette waddled from the porch to the truck. She looked as if she might pop any minute. "When's the due date again?" Wyatt asked.

"The doctor said she could go into labor as early as next week."

"Why don't you go with us to Joey's house?" Jaci asked Wyatt.

"Your mother and I are going to take a drive into town later so we can check on that new house you're going to be moving into."

A silver BMW pulled up in the driveway as Collette was buckling her seat belt.

"Ruthanne," Dylan said. "Perfect time for us to leave."

"We have to at least say hello," Collette said.

The "hellos" led to a lengthy monologue on how glad Ruthanne was to see Wyatt after so many years. He used the opportunity to size her up.

Rich. Attractive. Fake. That summed her up in his mind. If he had to guess, he'd bet the wealth and maybe some political clout was what had led to Riley's jilting Kelly's mother.

The senator had been a conniver even then. Wyatt itched to get back on his mother's murder case. If Riley Foley was behind Helene's murder, Wyatt would see that he paid. But even a death penalty wouldn't begin to compensate for the life he'd stolen from Helene and the years he'd stolen from Troy. It wouldn't begin to pay for the heartbreak of five boys who'd grown up without their mother or their father.

"I don't want to keep you," Ruthanne finally said. "Is Troy around?"

"Yes, but he's busy," Dylan said. "He said he didn't want to be disturbed."

Fast thinking on Dylan's part. Troy would owe him.

"We gotta git goin'," Jaci said, voicing what they were all thinking.

"So where are you off to, Jaci?" Ruthanne asked.

"We're going to Joey's house. Momma can't go, 'cause she's going to see our new house."

"That's nice."

Ruthanne finally walked back to her own car. Jaci waved as Dylan pulled away in his truck. And Wyatt went back inside to join Kelly in a little bit of afternoon delight.

There was a late-night bikers' bar on the other side of the county line where someone had told him this morning that Jerome occasionally hung out.

If Jerome showed up tonight, it would be his last night out for quite a while.

KELLY FELT A SURGE OF EXCITEMENT as she and Wyatt walked to the front door of the Callister house. In spite of Wyatt's fears, she refused to let herself believe that she was on a hit list ordered by Emanuel Leaky. Jerome was just a sick monster who was stalking her for some perverted reason of his own.

To believe that Emanuel wanted her dead was to give up any chance of ever living a normal life.

She had to hold on to the fact that Jerome would be arrested soon and she'd move into this adorable cottage and go on with her life—hopefully with Wyatt in it.

Wyatt opened the door and waited for her to step inside. She looked around, shocked at how naked the house looked with much of its interior ripped away. "It's like bones stripped of meat," she said.

"Picture it with the meat back on it. If we tear out that wall that separates this room from the kitchen, raise the ceiling by two feet and make that side wall a line of windows, this room would appear twice as large."

She visualized the changes, the same way she did when reworking a piece of old jewelry. Weigh what you'd lose from the old design against what you'd gain from the new. But if they did this right, she could keep the cottage feel of the house and not feel closed in.

"I think it's a great idea. I'll work with Dylan on the—"

A scraping noise that sounded as if it had come from the hallway interrupted her. "What was that?"

Wyatt's hand flew to the butt of the gun he'd worn at his waist ever since being deputized. "Stay back while I check it out.

"Foley. What happened here?"

Wyatt's question was followed by a noise that sounded like someone beating a sledgehammer against the wall. Kelly ran to the shadowed hallway.

Wyatt was on the floor, blood streaming from a huge gash on his head. His eyes were rolled back in his head and he wasn't moving.

"So nice to see you again, Kelly. Now we'll have lots of time to talk about Linda Ann."

Chapter Sixteen

"Ruthanne?"

"Yes, it's me. And, yes, I know all about your mother's tawdry affair with Riley." Her dark, accusing eyes stared back at Kelly, and the pistol she held in both hands was pointed at Kelly's head.

Fear rolled inside Kelly, so overpowering that her legs could barely hold her up. She couldn't think clearly. None of this made sense.

Wyatt still wasn't moving. Was he dead?

No, he couldn't be. She wouldn't let him be. She had to find a way to save them both.

"Tie Wyatt up, Jerome, and make quick work of it," Ruthanne ordered. "We need to finish this and clear out of here before McGuire or one of his hapless deputies come nosing around again."

Kelly spotted Jerome then, and he looked at her in that same perverted way he had when leaving the truck stop.

"I told you we'd meet again. Even I didn't expect it to be quite like this."

Her insides rolled. "You're depraved."

He laughed as if she'd paid him a compliment.

Finally she spotted the source of the scraping noise

that had become louder still. Riley was a few feet farther down the hallway, gagged and bound, writhing on the floor. Blood oozed from his mouth and puddled near his chest.

Kelly looked away from the gory sight. She had to focus. "You are in this with Jerome? Why, Ruthanne? None of this was about you. It was Riley who broke all the rules."

"Riley did nothing on his own except chase skirts. I made him who he is. I put up the money for his campaigns and used my family's clout to get him into all the right political circles. His thanks for that was leaving me."

More likely, he'd left her because she was crazy.

Wyatt was still out cold, but now Kelly could see the claw hammer lying by his feet. That must be what Jerome had hit him with.

Jerome tied Wyatt's ankles and bound his hands behind his back. He took Wyatt's gun from his holster and kicked it toward Ruthanne. "Want me to shoot the bitch for you or do you plan to stand here and talk all day?"

"Shut up, Jerome. I'm the one in charge here. The last time I trusted you with a murder, you fumbled it so badly, I had to do it myself."

"I didn't fumble it. You just couldn't wait for me to execute my plan."

"I don't want Kelly shot. I want her alive to feel the heat of the fire when this house goes up in flames and she's reduced to ashes. Too bad her adulterous mother can't be here to enjoy the occasion with her. Pour the gasoline all through the house now. We've wasted enough time."

"Consider it done." He laughed as he walked away.

Kelly struggled through the growing panic to get her mind around the truth. "So you know about my mother's affair with Riley?"

"Does that surprise you?"

"Did Helene Ledger tell you?"

"No. I made certain that self-righteous busybody never had the chance to tell me or anyone else."

"It was you who killed Helene Ledger," Kelly said as the obvious suddenly resonated through the confusion.

"I had no choice."

"But you were best friends. She was trying to help. She confronted Riley and was going to force him to confess the affair..." The illicit affair with Kelly's mother. How could that have led to murder and now to this?

The answer was tragically clear. Ruthanne was crazy and ruthless and vengeful beyond belief. Still...

Wyatt's body jerked and his eyes appeared to focus. He was alive. Relief flooded through Kelly though she knew that if she didn't do something fast, neither she, Wyatt or Riley would be alive for long.

She wondered if Ruthanne's confession had penetrated his comalike state and stirred him back to consciousness.

Ruthanne's finger curled around the trigger. "I prefer not to shoot you, Kelly, but make one move and I'll pull the trigger."

Being shot would be far better than burning to death, but she couldn't give up. Maybe the sheriff and his deputies would show up just as Ruthanne had said.

The smell of gasoline wafted though the house and Kelly's eyes and throat began to burn.

Wyatt began to writhe in pain just as Riley had been

doing a few minutes ago. No. Even in her peripheral vision she could tell that Wyatt's movements were more purposeful.

He was trying to free his hands from the rope. She had to keep Ruthanne talking. Wyatt needed time and they were fast running out of it.

"Why kill Helene?" Kelly asked again.

"She didn't merely want Riley to confess his indiscretions to me. She wanted him to admit his sins to the voters. Helene was a stickler for morality. She believed politicians should adhere to some higher standard than the rest of us."

Almost everyone adhered to a higher moral standard than Ruthanne. "Did having Riley elected mean that much to you?"

"Having Riley elected meant everything to me. If his chances of winning the election were off the table, he would have divorced me and married Linda Ann. I made sure that not only did he get elected but that he didn't dare leave me without being the number-one suspect in Helene's murder."

"And then you stood back and let Troy Ledger go to prison for your crime?"

"No. I didn't leave anything to chance. I packed Helene's bags that day after I killed her with Troy's gun. I ripped off her clothes so that if Troy did somehow prove his innocence, McGuire would never suspect a woman of the crime."

"You'll never get away with this."

"Of course I will. Jerome will bear all the blame. He won't mind. He'll be in Rio de Janeiro. The transportation is already arranged."

Ruthanne's voice grew husky from the fumes.

"All done," Jerome said. "I'm to the bottom of the

last can." He walked over and stood next to Wyatt, then let the remaining drops of fuel drip onto Wyatt's shirt.

"I'm leaving now," Ruthanne said. "Tie up Kelly and then stand outside and listen for my car to start and drive away from the trees, where I hid it, before you fire up this incinerator."

"Nice knowing you, Wyatt," Ruthanne said as if she was merely driving away as she'd done when leaving the ranch this afternoon. "Give my regards to your mother and tell her I plan to marry the poor grieving husband she left behind."

Ruthanne turned and started walking to the back door. This was it. Kelly and Wyatt would die together. She'd never again feel his arms around her. She wouldn't be there to see Jaci grow up.

Tears burned at the back of her eyes as Jerome bound her. Even bound, she might be able to worm her way to the door but not before Jerome dropped the match and created the inferno. There was no way to save herself or Wyatt.

"I love you, Wyatt. I love you with all my heart. I wanted to spend the rest of my life with you and Jaci. I wanted that so very, very much."

Jerome crammed a gag into her mouth and walked away.

Chapter Seventeen

Wyatt's hand slipped from the last knot just as Jerome stepped over him. He grabbed one of Jerome's legs and yanked so hard that Jerome's head bounced off the hall-way wall as he fell to the floor beside Wyatt. His gun went flying across the floor.

Wyatt's ankles were still tied. His only chance was to keep Jerome pinned to the floor. If Jerome managed to get back on his feet, Wyatt might not be able to stop him before he escaped the house and ignited the gasoline.

No way could Wyatt let this house go up in flames with Kelly inside. He had to buy her time to escape. Adrenaline pumped through him like a water jet. His instincts and training ruled his brain and his muscles. He tore the gag from his mouth.

"Get out, Kelly. Roll to the back door or hold on to the wall and hop. Just get out now!"

Jerome planted an elbow jab to Wyatt's neck, but Wyatt maintained his grip as Jerome regrouped, coming back with a knee to Wyatt's crotch.

Kelly was moving, but in the wrong direction. She was coming toward him and Jerome. Jerome had his back to her, but he'd never let her get past them.

And then he saw Kelly's foot brush up against Jerome's gun. She kicked it toward Wyatt. It stopped a few inches short of his reach.

Wyatt heard the back door open. No doubt Ruthanne back to check out the delay. Ruthanne had a gun, and she might not realize that gunfire might be all it took to send the house up in flames.

Wyatt shoved with every ounce of strength in his body. He moved the deadlock of his and Jerome's entwined bodies just enough to fit his hand around the butt of the gun. He punched the barrel into Jerome's side.

"If I pull this trigger, we may all light up the sky," Wyatt said.

"That's not certain."

"Are you willing to chance it?"

Jerome's face turned a pasty white and sweat poured down his face as if he'd just climbed out of the shower.

Wyatt heard heavy footsteps coming from the front of the house. Jerome broke free and started to run out the back.

McGuire stamped into the hallway. "Dad burn it to hell and back. This house has more gasoline than Exxon. What kind of party are you guys throwing?"

Relief swept through Wyatt but it was short-lived.

"Jerome's got matches and more fuel to spread. We're going to blow."

"Jerome's wearing a nice little metal bracelet by now. My deputies got him before he made it out the door to finish his dirty work." Then he called out to another deputy who'd entered the house. "Brent, carry Kelly out and don't stop until she's clear of explosions danger. Charlie, do the same with... Hell, that's the senator. Get him out of here, too."

McGuire had already stooped and slit the ropes that bound Wyatt's ankles.

Wyatt staggered a bit as he stood.

"Lean on me, Wyatt," McGuire ordered. "We gotta move. It won't take much to make kindling and ashes of this house."

Squad cars and fire trucks were pouring into the driveway by the time they got outside.

Wyatt was still a bit woozy and a hen egg was forming on the side of his head. It would have been a lot worse if hadn't grabbed Jerome's arm in time to lessen the blow.

He looked around for Kelly and spotted her surrounded by deputies at the far end of the long driveway. To his amazement, he spotted Ruthanne, too, also surrounded by deputies.

"I want you and Kelly both to get checked over at the hospital. A police order," McGuire said, before he could protest. "I'll catch up with you there and take your statements."

"That was great timing on your part," Wyatt said. "How did you manage it?"

"Good police work. I've had deputies periodically checking the wooded area behind Kelly's house just in case Jerome was lying in wait back there. When I saw the cars, I called for backup. And then we ran into Ruthanne, trying to make a fast getaway. I figured she had to be involved."

"She admitted to killing my mother."

"You're kidding."

"No. It's a long and very complicated story. I'll feed you all the details, but first I need to make sure Kelly is all right."

"But you say Ruthanne confessed to killing Helene?"

"Yes. She was talking to Kelly, but I heard. Of course, she was expecting both of us to die before we could repeat it."

"Under the circumstances, I think you should perform one final duty as a deputy."

"What's that?"

"Go arrest Ruthanne Foley for the murder of Helene Ledger."

"I think I can handle that task."

KELLY WAS STANDING not two feet away when Wyatt read Ruthanne her rights and slipped the handcuffs on her wrists. She knew he'd lived for this moment since he was thirteen and had come home to find his mother's body stretched out on the floor.

A few minutes ago she'd thought their lives were over. Now life lay before them like a road paved with golden promise. All they had to do was take it.

She'd told him how she felt. The rest was up to Wyatt. She'd give him all the time he needed. She wasn't going anywhere.

When he finished making the arrest, the sheriff led Ruthanne to a waiting squad car.

Wyatt came over and took her in his arms. "I've faced killers more times than I can count," Wyatt said. "I've never been as afraid as I was tonight when I thought I might not be able to save you." His voice was husky with emotion.

"But you did save me, Wyatt. You saved both of us and the senator."

"Yeah, but there's something we should clear up here and now."

"I can't think of anything that can't wait."

"I can. Remember what you said when you thought we were goners?"

"That I love you."

"That you wanted to spend the rest of your life with me."

"You don't have to—"

"Don't go backing out now. I know a proposal when I hear one and that was definitely a proposal. My answer is yes."

"Oh, Wyatt, I love you."

"I love you, too, Kelly. I've never been more certain of anything in my life. "

He kissed her and her world that had veered so wrong became right again.

Epilogue

Three months later

Troy stood at the back of the courtyard garden and took in the happiness that surrounded him for Wyatt and Kelly's wedding.

Tyler was home from Afghanistan for good and would be working the ranch with him and Dylan. Eve had just a little bump beneath her new dress. Joey would be getting a sibling in the fall. Collette had given birth to a strapping boy that they'd named after Troy.

Dakota was going back to school in the fall to pursue a degree in equine veterinary medicine. Wyatt and Kelly had moved into the old Callister house, though they were still working on the new wing. And Wyatt was in charge of the new homicide division of the local sheriff's department.

Notwithstanding the seventeen years he'd spent in prison, Troy was incredibly blessed. He'd married the woman he loved and she'd given him these five wonderful sons. He cherished every memory he had of the time he'd shared with Helene. He missed her so much at times like these, he could barely stand it.

Helene should be here today. She should be sharing

this moment with Wyatt and Kelly. She should be delighting in her grandchildren and holding Dylan's son close to her heart while she sang him a lullaby the way she had their boys.

Lately, he couldn't seem to find her when he walked in the garden in a cold mist or even in the glimmer of moonlight. But he could always find Helene in his heart.

Wyatt walked up to him. "You still miss Mom, don't you?"

"I'll always miss her, but life goes on. I am a very blessed man."

"In spite of the years you spent in prison?"

"I should have fought harder for my freedom. I should have done that for you boys. But I couldn't get past the grief. That's not an excuse. It's how it was."

"I know. I've finally forgiven myself for not being able to hold the family together in your absence."

"You had nothing to forgive yourself for. You were a fine son then, Wyatt. You still are. You were our first-born. You made us a family." Troy put an arm around Wyatt's shoulder. "Now you'll have a family of your own, and I have no doubt that you'll be a wonderful husband and father."

"Thanks, *Dad*. And in case I haven't said it, I love you."

"I love you, too, son." Troy backhanded a lone, salty tear from the corner of his eye as Wyatt walked away.

Jaci ran up and tugged on his hand. "C'mon, Grandpa. We gotta git goin'. You have to see me throw those torn up roses on the ground for Momma to step on."

WYATT STOOD beneath the arch of flowers and looked down at his beautiful bride. From the most tragic day of his life to the happiest. Things had gone full circle here on Willow Creek Ranch.

Life was neither fair nor predictable. But right now it was as good as it got. Justice had finally been served for his mother. His father's name had been cleared. Sadly, Senator Foley had not survived the gunshot wound to his chest, so Kelly would never get to decide for herself whether or not she wanted him in her life.

But Ruthanne was in jail awaiting trial for Helene's and Riley's murders. Jerome Hurley was in jail, as well. There had been nothing to indicate that Emanuel Leaky was planning revenge against Kelly or even knew that she'd been instrumental in his arrest.

And hard-nosed, loner cop Wyatt Ledger was about to gain a daughter and a wife he loved more than he'd ever thought possible.

"Wyatt Ledger, do you take Kelly Burger to be your lawfully wedded wife to live together in marriage? Do you promise to love, comfort, honor and keep her for better or worse, for richer or poorer, in sickness and in health, and forsaking all others, be faithful only to her so long as you both shall live?"

"I do." It was the easiest promise he'd ever made.

"YOU MAY KISS THE BRIDE."

Kelly felt the promises of a million tomorrows in Wyatt's kiss. She'd never dreamed she could be this happy.

As the wedding march started, her thoughts turned

to the woman who'd given birth to the marvelous man Kelly loved so deeply.

Rest in peace, Helene Ledger. The sons of you and Troy Ledger have all come home to stay.

* * * * *

SUSPENSE

Heartstopping stories of intrigue and mystery—
where true love always triumphs.

Harlequin®

INTRIGUE®

COMING NEXT MONTH
AVAILABLE FEBRUARY 14 2012

#1329 COWBOY IN THE EXTREME
Bucking Bronc Lodge
Rita Herron

#1330 SCENE OF THE CRIME: MYSTIC LAKE
Carla Cassidy

#1331 THE LOST GIRLS OF JOHNSON'S BAYOU
Jana DeLeon

#1332 SUDDEN ATTRACTION
Mindbenders
Rebecca York

#1333 POWER OF THE RAVEN
Copper Canyon
Aimée Thurlo

#1334 HER COWBOY DEFENDER
Thriller
Kerry Connor

You can find more information on upcoming Harlequin® titles,
free excerpts and more at www.HarlequinInsideRomance.com.

HICNM0112

REQUEST YOUR FREE BOOKS!
2 FREE NOVELS PLUS 2 FREE GIFTS!

Harlequin®

INTRIGUE®

BREATHTAKING ROMANTIC SUSPENSE

YES! Please send me 2 FREE Harlequin Intrigue® novels and my 2 FREE gifts (gifts are worth about $10). After receiving them, if I don't wish to receive any more books, I can return the shipping statement marked "cancel." If I don't cancel, I will receive 6 brand-new novels every month and be billed just $4.49 per book in the U.S. or $5.24 per book in Canada. That's a saving of at least 14% off the cover price! It's quite a bargain! Shipping and handling is just 50¢ per book in the U.S. and 75¢ per book in Canada.* I understand that accepting the 2 free books and gifts places me under no obligation to buy anything. I can always return a shipment and cancel at any time. Even if I never buy another book, the two free books and gifts are mine to keep forever.

182/382 HDN FEQ2

Name	(PLEASE PRINT)	

Address		Apt. #

City	State/Prov.	Zip/Postal Code

Signature (if under 18, a parent or guardian must sign)

Mail to the **Reader Service:**
IN U.S.A.: P.O. Box 1867, Buffalo, NY 14240-1867
IN CANADA: P.O. Box 609, Fort Erie, Ontario L2A 5X3

Not valid for current subscribers to Harlequin Intrigue books.

**Are you a subscriber to Harlequin Intrigue books
and want to receive the larger-print edition?
Call 1-800-873-8635 or visit www.ReaderService.com.**

* Terms and prices subject to change without notice. Prices do not include applicable taxes. Sales tax applicable in N.Y. Canadian residents will be charged applicable taxes. Offer not valid in Quebec. This offer is limited to one order per household. All orders subject to credit approval. Credit or debit balances in a customer's account(s) may be offset by any other outstanding balance owed by or to the customer. Please allow 4 to 6 weeks for delivery. Offer available while quantities last.

Your Privacy—The Reader Service is committed to protecting your privacy. Our Privacy Policy is available online at www.ReaderService.com or upon request from the Reader Service.

We make a portion of our mailing list available to reputable third parties that offer products we believe may interest you. If you prefer that we not exchange your name with third parties, or if you wish to clarify or modify your communication preferences, please visit us at www.ReaderService.com/consumerschoice or write to us at Reader Service Preference Service, P.O. Box 9062, Buffalo, NY 14269. Include your complete name and address.

HI11B

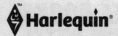
Harlequin®

n o c t u r n e™

NEW YORK TIMES AND *USA TODAY*
BESTSELLING AUTHOR

RACHEL LEE

captivates with another installment of

The Claiming

When Yvonne Dupuis gets a creepy sensation that
someone is watching her, waiting in the shadows,
she turns to Messenger Investigations and finds herself
under the protection of vampire Creed Preston.
His hunger for her is extreme, but with evil lurking
at every turn Creed must protect Yvonne from the
demonic forces that are trying to capture her
and claim her for his own.

CLAIMED BY A VAMPIRE

Available in February wherever books are sold.

HN61876

*Louisa Morgan loves being around children.
So when she has the opportunity to tutor bedridden Ellie,
she's determined to bring joy back into the motherless
girl's world. Can she also help Ellie's father open his
heart again? Read on for a sneak peek of*

THE COWBOY FATHER

*by Linda Ford,
available February 2012 from Love Inspired Historical.*

Why had Louisa thought she could do this job? A bubble of self-pity whispered she was totally useless, but Louisa ignored it. She wasn't useless. She could help Ellie if the child allowed it.

Emmet walked her out, waiting until they were out of earshot to speak. "I sense you and Ellie are not getting along."

"Ellie has lost her freedom. On top of that, everything is new. Familiar things are gone. Her only defense is to exert what little independence she has left. I believe she will soon tire of it and find there are more enjoyable ways to pass the time."

He looked doubtful. Louisa feared he would tell her not to return. But after several seconds' consideration, he sighed heavily. "You're right about one thing. She's lost everything. She can hardly be blamed for feeling out of sorts."

"She hasn't lost everything, though." Her words were quiet, coming from a place full of certainty that Emmet was more than enough for this child. "She has you."

"She'll always have me. As long as I live." He clenched his fists. "And I fully intend to raise her in such a way that even if something happened to me, she would never feel like I was gone. I'd be in her thoughts and in her actions every day."

Peace filled Louisa. "Exactly what my father did."

Their gazes connected, forged a single thought about fathers and daughters…how each needed the other. How sweet the relationship was.

Louisa tipped her head away first. "I'll see you tomorrow."

Emmet nodded. "Until tomorrow then."

She climbed behind the wheel of their automobile and turned toward home. She admired Emmet's devotion to his child. It reminded her of the love her own father had lavished on Louisa and her sisters. Louisa smiled as fond memories of her father filled her thoughts. Ellie was a fortunate child to know such love.

Louisa understands what both father and daughter are going through. Will her compassion help them heal—and form a new family? Find out in
THE COWBOY FATHER
by Linda Ford, available February 14, 2012.

Love Inspired Books celebrates 15 years of inspirational romance in 2012! February puts the spotlight on Love Inspired Historical, with each book celebrating family and the special place it has in our hearts. Be sure to pick up all four Love Inspired Historical stories, available February 14, wherever books are sold.

Copyright © 2012 by Linda Ford

SHLIHEXP0212